Fifty Algae Stories

of Hope, Health, and Freedom

Lisa C. Moore, DC

Ransom Hill Press

Ransom Hill Press
PO Box 325
Ramona, California 92065-0325

Cover art by Amanda Schaffer.
Production, interior layout and cover design by Summer Andrecht.

Library of Congress Catalog Card Number: 96-072084
ISBN 0-941903-18-4

Second Printing

Acknowledgment

Without the wonderful stories, there would be no book, so first thanks belong to the many people who allowed me into their lives. Hopefully, their examples will inspire others to change their lives through superfood nutrition.

Thanks to Polly Meyers of Ransom Hill Press for taking a risk with an unknown author and an unwritten product, and to Summer Andrecht for her diplomacy and patience.

A special thank you to Daryl and Marta Kollman and their family for never giving up. Ever!

Much gratitude to my upline and my downline in Cell Tech, the Auburn Distributor Empowerment Team, and to my sponsor, Dorothy Zelle, for cheering me on and supporting me in the creation of this project.

And last, but definitely not least, my love and appreciation to my two children, Christopher and Laura, for putting up with my long hours on the computer and telephone, hastily prepared meals, and the never ending chorus, "Not until I'm done with my book!" Well kids, now I'm done!

Disclaimer

Cell Tech is a direct marketing company that provides nutritional and personal care products to consumers through independent distributors. Each distributorship is neither a franchise nor an exclusive distributorship, nor are distributors employees of Cell Tech. The edible products provided by Cell Tech are considered foods and are not to be confused with medicine or drugs of any type.

Stories in this book were submitted by independent Cell Tech distributors. They are for informational purposes only, and do not constitute medical claims as to the cure, prevention, mitigation, or treatment of any disease, nor do they supply medical advice. All claims are nutritional only and have not been evaluated by the Federal Food and Drug Administration.

The author is not an employee of Cell Tech. This book was written independently of Cell Tech, but has been approved by Cell Tech for general dissemination to the public.

The following phrases are trademarked by Cell Tech: Energy for Life™, Alpha Sun™, Omega Sun™, Spectrabiotic™, Super Blue Green™ Algae, Energy for Fun™, and Energy for Change™.

Cell Tech approval number 99750.

Contents

Note to the Reader

The following stories have endured the rigorous Cell Tech approval process. Inherent in this journey is the removal of disease names, diagnoses, and many descriptive words that might suggest a medical claim. Because of this process, some of the stories may not be as detailed or as impactive as they might be otherwise. The author suggests that the creative reader use his or her imagination to infer any embellishment that might seem appropriate. Enjoy!

Preface

I was eighteen when I went off to chiropractic college. I had been raised in a middle class family with traditional medical ideas. My father's company provided us free, unlimited access to physicians, surgeons, pharmaceuticals, and hospital facilities. If we became ill, we saw a doctor. Once in a while the doctor even came to us. Fortunately, my parents were also open-minded, intelligent seekers who occasionally branched out to look for alternatives. My visit to a chiropractor after a gymnastics fall peaked my interest in natural healing.

In chiropractic college, I learned that the human body contains an inborn ability to heal and regenerate. We call it Innate Intelligence. This inner wisdom needs no help, just no interference. It ensures that every organ, tissue, and cell performs at its maximum capacity. It also knows when to heal, what to heal, and how to heal.

I was truly amazed! With minimal help from outside sources, our miraculous bodies can heal themselves. Disease doesn't come from outside of us, and neither does wellness. But we do have some control over the external influences that affect our ability to be the best we can be. These elements include:

1. Adequate exercise
2. Sufficient and regular sleep
3. Positive mental attitude
4. Fresh air and clean water
5. Whole, balanced, minimally processed foods
6. Rest and relaxation

Of course, in my profession, we also recognize the importance of structural and neurological integrity. The nervous system plays a major role in our ability to heal. As my chiropractic approach has evolved further along the path of allowing the body to repair itself with minimal outside help, so has my nutritional philosophy.

I quickly discovered that whole food supplementation provides the necessary building blocks for cellular rejuvenation and that removing active ingredients in a laboratory and re-combining them in a test tube cannot and does not produce a viable material able to sustain life. Even vitamins and miner-als extracted from a natural source and mixed with other par-tial substances do not perform the same way as they do in their foods of origin. Scientists continually discover new trace elements that are necessary for the optimum usage of other more common nutrients. It is often the balance between these substances that provides the magic combination that the body requires. One isolated vitamin, mineral, or portion thereof is not an adequate substitute for the whole food. Megavitamin therapy may provide slight benefit in correcting long stand-ing deficiencies, but clinical nutritionists are aware that eat-ing whole foods in as natural a state as possible is the ideal way to nourish the body. Because tissues and organs need ad-equate raw materials to perform their designated tasks, nu-tritional deficiency is often a major contributor to organic mal-function and disease.

This is where Super Blue Green Algae comes in. Every member of my practice who has included the algae in his or her health care program has noticed an improvement in his or her body's ability to respond to adjustments and experi-enced increased overall feelings of "aliveness." By adding a wild-grown, whole food to their previously deficient diets, some people have seen a reduction in fatigue or an improve-ment in long standing health problems. These are not miracle cures. Without nutritional fuel, the body's basic internal pro-cesses function inadequately, and energy cannot be produced at the cellular level. Food putrefies and pollutes our bodies instead of providing nourishment. Glands become overloaded and can no longer filter waste products efficiently. The im-mune system breaks down, and eventually, the body turns on itself.

The following stories cover a variety of deficiencies and illustrate a broad range of changes in people's lives with the addition of this incredible food. Super Blue Green Algae is a priceless gift at a time in the evolution of our planet when we badly need help. Perhaps with improvements in agricultural practices and the advancement of conscious wellness care, we human beings (and our animal friends) will no longer need to turn to an obscure blue-green algae for nourishment.

At this time in history, we should be grateful for the bounty of Klamath Lake, and to the Kollmans and Cell Tech for bringing it to us. Thank you, Daryl and Marta, for all that you do and all that you are.

Dr. Lisa Moore
Auburn, California

"Algae offer us an opportunity to participate in the dignity of the earth — her beauty, grandeur, roughness, wildness — and to reconnect with those qualities in ourselves. Because of its harmonious vibrational configuration and high energy potential, Super Blue Green Algae is so potentially powerful that it can dramatically shift the health and consciousness of all those who partake of its life-giving properties."

— *Optocrystallization Patterns: A Report of the Photographs Showing the Vibrational Properties of Freshwater Algae,* 1994. (Available through Cell Tech.)

Tell Me About Algae

What is Super Blue Green Algae?

Super Blue Green Algae is a trade name for Aphanizomenon flos-aquae, a strain of blue-green algae which grows abundantly in Klamath Lake in Oregon. Several companies harvest this nutrient dense food, but only Cell Tech uses the name Super Blue Green.

Like other types of blue-green algae, this life form has survived on our planet since the dawn of time. Through the miracle of photosynthesis, it was the first organism to release free oxygen into the air, giving life to our atmosphere, and making it earth's first food. Algae are responsible for 90% of all the oxygen we breathe. Trees and other plants contribute only 10%.

A key component in the photosynthesis process, and the secret to the algae's ability to convert sunlight to energy, is a molecule called chlorophyll. Algae contain more chlorophyll by weight than any other plants on earth. This substance provides a variety of benefits for the body, one of which is a cleansing action. Much like a giant broom, the chlorophyll in Super Blue Green Algae sweeps out toxic buildup from tissues and organs. It also aids in digestion, and because of its similarity to the hemoglobin molecule, chlorophyll supports red blood cell formation and increases the oxygen carrying capacity of blood.

Other attributes of this amazing food:

• Aphanizomenon flos-aquae is a superior plant source of Vitamin B12, which is essential to red blood cell formation and may be deficient in vegetarian diets.

• Super Blue Green Algae supplies the building blocks for neuropeptides that are "essential for nervous system functions such as concentration, moods, sleep, pain perception, etc."*

• Antioxidants, such as the beta carotene contained in Super Blue Green Algae, assist the body in eliminating damaging free radicals caused by pollution, radiation, sunlight, and toxic chemicals that speed up the aging process and damage our tissues.

• Super Blue Green Algae includes most of the vitamins and minerals the body requires. It also provides us with all nine essential amino acids in a near perfect ratio. These amino acids are utilized in the synthesis of protein and must be obtained from an outside source because they are not produced by our bodies.

• While most plants have cellulose cell walls, this type of algae has a glycolipoprotein cell wall, an easily digestible source of energy.

• Super Blue Green Algae is enzyme active, meaning it contains high levels of life giving properties which aid in the digestive process.

• Ongoing research verifies that colors affect the neurological frequency of the body in different ways. Christian Drapeau, head of Research and Development for Cell Tech, emphasizes the healing properties of the color green. In a lecture he gave in Klamath Falls in August 1995, Mr. Drapeau pointed out that frequency can change the whole pattern of the body.

Why algae? Why now?

Over the last fifty years, the topsoil in our country and in most countries of the world has become so badly depleted

---

* Christian Drapeau, MSc., *The Physiology of the Algae*. Klamath Falls: Cell Tech, 1994. Only available as a book and audiotape combination.

that it can no longer provide the diversity of nutrients that plants need to be healthy. Modern farming methods require that many crops be repeatedly planted in the same soil over and over again. Breakthroughs in fertilizer production have created the ability to mass produce great quantities of chemical supplementation for less money, and farmers rely upon pesticides to eliminate the threat of hungry bugs destroying precious crops. But at what cost?

Chemical fertilizers generally replace only three of the many necessary elements that are removed from the earth by growing plants. Previously, organic farming methods and crop rotation ensured that our soil was allowed to replenish itself before being called upon to sustain another round of growth. Cover crops that are tilled back into the earth also supply valuable ingredients. Most chemical fertilizers provide only nitrogen, phosphorous and potassium, which cause fruits and vegetables to look as they should, even though these foods contain less than a fraction of the vitamins and minerals our bodies need to replenish and rebuild themselves. Plants can't provide what they don't contain.

Aphanizomenon flos-aquae grow in a nutrient-rich lake that receives runoff from the Cascade mountains. Thirty-five feet of organic sediment on the bottom of the lake provides enough nourishment for the algae to grow for hundreds of years, even if the sediment were never replenished. Fortunately, runoff from the surrounding mountains continuously brings more minerals down through rivers and springs, so the algae has a never ending supply of nutrient rich food.

What *is* information rich *food?*

According to Mr. Daryl Kollman, CEO of Cell Tech, the information contained in Super Blue Green Algae is "the foundation for all of life. Said another way, all the other information known by all other living things is stored in the algae."*

---

* Daryl Kollman, *Hope is a Molecule.* Klamath Falls: Cell Tech, 1989. This article is available in the winter 1989 issue of "New Leaf" magazine.

Because blue-green algae were the first organic life to develop on this planet, they have learned to survive and thrive, which means they also contain genes for hardiness.

Cellular memory is usually kept locked inside the nucleus of a cell and is shared only upon cellular division. However, because algae have no nuclei, they operate much like bacteria. Their structure allows for a free flow of information between cells, including the cells of your digestive tract. Recent scientific studies have shown that bacteria "constantly update the information they exchange, such as adjusting to changes in the environment, by sharing genes (information) with each other."[*] Therefore, any knowledge the algae posses is now shared with anyone or anything that ingests them. As Daryl Kollman says with awe, "You just ate 3.5 billion years of constantly updated, fundamental information about the essence of life itself. Talk about 'on line'! Wow!"[†]

How can food make such a difference in people's lives?

The foregoing might lead one to believe that algae is a panacea. The real miracle of Super Blue Green Algae is that it is here for us now at a time when we badly need a source of food that is not dependent upon our anemic topsoil for subsistence. It lives and grows as a wild food that does not require human beings to supply it with a medium for growth. Nature provides the habitat and nourishment for Aphanizomenon flos-aquae: manna from deep inside the earth for sustenance and over three hundred days a year of sunlight to encourage its reproduction.

Many of the illnesses from which man has suffered throughout the ages are a direct result of a faulty diet that either lacks required nutrients or contains too many empty and toxic substitutes. Nutrition charts outline basic vitamins and minerals and recount a litany of deficiency diseases that

---

[*] Daryl Kollman, *Hope is a Molecule*. Klamath Falls: Cell Tech, 1989. This article is available in the winter 1989 issue of "New Leaf" magazine.
[†] Ibid., Daryl Kollman, 1989.

result from their absence. However, it is important to point out that balance is most often the key to maintaining a healthy internal environment. Vitamins, minerals, and trace elements all work together in harmony to ensure health and wellness. It isn't enough to make sure that we have isolated nutrients, especially if they come from a chemical source. Foods in nature are combined in a specific manner that allows for their optimum assimilation and vital activity. A minuscule amount of some nutrients in combination with a few other necessary components may be all that is required to catalyze a reaction or maintain function in the human body.

When scientists discover that a certain vitamin or mineral prevents an associated disease, they often ignore the fact that the vitamin or mineral lives with other nutrients that work in concert with it. These chemical wizards isolate particular substances, remove them from the food in which they are found, and then expect them to function identically on their own. The next step is to synthetically recreate the "active" ingredient, call it *Vitamin XYZ*, and claim that it performs exactly as nature's food. Clinical nutritionists know that nature and the human body don't function in this manner.

Food doesn't cure anything.

And neither does Super Blue Green Algae. However, it is a wild-grown, naturally produced food that can provide your body with a complete and balanced source of nutrients that fill in the gap left by hollow, and sometimes chemically altered, supermarket fare. It contains a vitality that feeds the life-force within us and also within our special animal friends. There is nothing else like it on the planet.

The stories inside this book give a glimpse of the changes that can occur in people's lives when good nutrition realigns bodies that are out of balance. Perhaps you, too, could benefit from adding Super Blue Green Algae to your diet. Please join us on the road back to health.

1

Children's Stories

"You can consciously change the energy and informational content of your own quantum mechanical body, and therefore influence the energy and informational content of your extended body — your environment, your world — and cause things to manifest in it."

— From the book <u>The Seven Spiritual Laws of Success</u> © 1994 Deepak Chopra. Reprinted by permission of Amber-Allen Publishing, Inc. P.O. Box 6657, San Rafael, CA 94903. All rights reserved.

Noah Carter

Noah is a thirteen year old, seventh grade boy living in Paso Robles, California. Since first grade, he has had challenges in the areas of attention, focus, concentration, and learning. He often forgot to turn in his papers and bring his books home. Nevertheless, Noah's parents discontinued his medication approximately a year ago because they were uncomfortable with the increasing dosages and the explosive behavior he exhibited at the end of each day as the medication wore off.

Noah Carter

A short year ago, Noah began eating Super Blue Green Algae with the EAT kit.* This program includes probiotics and enzymes for maximizing digestibility, and the algae, Omega[†] and Alpha Sun.[‡] After eating these products for two weeks, Noah brought home schoolwork with the teacher's remarks "Excellent!" and "Best in class!" scrawled across the top. He was so proud when he received the highest score out of all the seventh and eighth graders on a language test. Noah also began interacting better with his five year old brother, and even taught him how to play chess. His mother mentions that she enjoyed his company more. He seemed more pleasant, more willing to talk, and less withdrawn.

* See page 177 for information on the EAT Kit from Cell Tech.
[†] See page 174 for more information on Omega Sun Algae.
[‡] See page 174 for more information on Alpha Sun Algae.

During Noah's third and fourth weeks on Super Blue Green Algae, his teachers remarked that he was sitting at attention, raising his hand, and participating more in class. He even went to the library one day to check out a book about how to learn Spanish! His mother noticed that his change in attitude was like "night and day." Most importantly, Noah seemed happier.

After Noah had been eating the algae for two months, the school principal commented on Noah's improved disposition. His whole persona had changed: his moods and attitudes were balanced, and he no longer appeared somewhat depressed. Noah completed his homework over the school holiday without being asked, and spent less time glued to the television and/or Nintendo. On his own, he began learning a foreign language, and he entered a chess tournament.

Noah Carter continues to blossom because of his improved nutrition. He eats two Spectrabiotics,* four Super Blue Green Enzymes,† two Alpha Sun algae and four Omega Sun algae every day. All but the enzymes are consumed with breakfast, which seems to be just as effective for him as spacing them evenly throughout his day. "Noah's family is so thankful to have found that the results they have been seeking for years from modern medicine are available from a natural nutritional food source that has no adverse side effects," says family friend Kathryn.

Noah's counselor is now documenting his progress, and his mother has been inspired to create a support group in her community.

Kathryn Reid-Carriero
Auburn, California

---

* See page 175 for more information on Spectrabiotics.
† See page 175 for more information on Super Blue Green Enzymes.

T.J. Sonner

Following twenty-one hours of a long and difficult labor, Becki birthed her first child.

She was attending college full-time and riding the rough seas of a stormy marriage when she discovered she was pregnant with T.J. Overwhelming nausea during her first trimester, coupled with her heavy class load, had left her little time for her foundering marriage.

T.J. immediately became a challenge. His colic, quick temper and inability to nap for any length of time were the first indications of a highly sensitive, rambunctious little boy. He continued to exhibit heart-stopping fearlessness, intermittent aggression, and increasing irritability. One day, when T.J. could barely crawl, Becki found him atop the refrigerator exploring the cupboard above. Luckily, she rescued him just in time. After her daughter Brandee was born, Becki couldn't leave the two children in the same room for fear T.J. would hurt his baby sister. Mischievous but charming T.J. had metamorphosed into an angry, resentful older brother. Becki's marriage eventually broke under the strain, and T.J.'s parents divorced when he was five, his sister three.

Then came T.J.'s educational experiences. While her son was in preschool, Becki remembers holding her breath in anticipation at a school performance while T.J. struggled to participate. Other children danced, sang, and joined in the skits. *Her* child stared into the lights, rubbed his nose, tossed his head, and danced when everyone else was still. "To my dismay, I listened as strange bodily sounds [erupted] from his mouth," recalls Becki. Other parents whispered among themselves and wondered out loud who the disruptive child belonged to. Becki suffered in silence. When the performance concluded, T.J. ran to his mother with an irresistible sparkle in his eyes. Her heart melted. "How could I not love this child who was so full of it? Even though at times I didn't know what *it* was."

Fortunately for Becki, she met a wonderful, caring man whom she married not long after her divorce. T.J., of course, blamed himself for the failure of the first marriage, and his behavior deteriorated further.

This bright, charming, but active child became so frustrated with his inability to focus and accomplish his school work that he often threw temper tantrums. In first grade, he began banging his head on the desk while the entire class and their teacher looked on helplessly. Though his IQ tested at a high 136, T.J. was failing in school. The sadness he carried because of his desire to do well, and his inability to follow through, overwhelmed him. One day, on the way home from school in the car, T.J. turned to his mother with tears in his eyes. He told her that he wished he could drink enough alcohol to kill himself. School was too hard. T. J. couldn't cope.

One Mother's Day, his class teacher called Becki in to see the frightful picture he had drawn on his card for her. Tears welled up in Becki's eyes as she saw a picture of their house with T.J. standing beside it. He clutched a bloody knife in his hand and his heart dripped blood like sap from a tree. Underneath, T.J. had scrawled, "For Mother's Day, my gift to you is that I die so your life could be better." Thus, there followed an endless stream of counseling, behavior modification programs, medication, school meetings, tests, seminars, and other interventions, with very little improvement. He remained highly excitable, anxious, and easily overstimulated.

"Fire prevention week was a nightmare for T.J. He didn't sleep for two weeks straight, staying up at night so he could be sure and hear the fire alarm," recalls Becki. Late one night, a hysterical T.J. came running down the stairs, screaming that the fire alarm was ringing. It turned out to be the erratic beeping of a low battery in the smoke detector.

A simple childhood illness such as chicken pox drove T.J. crazy because of the interminable itching. Although Becki tried everything from wrapping his arms and legs to hugging him tightly, she couldn't dissuade him from scratching constantly. This left him with numerous scars.

By the time T.J. turned ten years old, his exhausted family

had tried every remedy they could think of to help him lead a normal life. When he developed severe motor dysfunction, specialists in Salt Lake City provided some help, but the emotional component remained. In October of that year, T.J. entered an institution. Becki's heart was breaking as she kissed her son good-bye. Determined not to lose him, she never gave up hope. For four weeks, T.J. underwent extensive testing. The results showed no detectable biological dysfunction in his brain. Yet the emotional problems persisted.

The doctors made changes in their treatment regimen, including the addition of a rigid behavior modification program, but they offered little hope of success. Their recommendation? — further institutionalization, which the Lindermans could not afford. The bleak prognosis was the possibility of future incarceration in a juvenile facility. Hope began to dwindle in the Linderman home, but Becki persevered.

At this point a close friend introduced her to Super Blue Green Algae. The night the first shipment arrived, T.J. asked to try the liquid Omega Sun. Shortly after taking a dropper full, this previously uncooperative, intractable boy jumped up out of his chair and began single-handedly to prepare the family dinner. He set the table, assembled the meal, and even washed the dishes afterward. Becki was amazed! When questioned, T.J. said, "I have all this energy, I might as well do something constructive with it." After cleaning up the dishes, T.J. inserted a cassette tape in his "boom box" and turned up the volume as he sang the answers to his math homework. A stunned mother could hardly believe her eyes.

She introduced T.J. to the algae products slowly, first using the enzymes, then adding the Omega and Alpha Sun. Progress was erratic but positive. T.J. experienced many symptoms of detoxification. At times, he seemed more hyperactive and initially had difficulty sleeping. Slight diarrhea and nausea dissipated after the first week. Becki varied the amount of algae she gave her son until she reached a level that seemed to work best for him.

Though it was a struggle, T.J. managed to finish the fifth grade. Becki discovered some alternative healing methods that complemented her nutritional work with T.J. He also began to meet with a psychologist who supported the family's unconventional approach. He saw T.J. as a gifted child who needed nourishment on many levels, not as a disturbed boy ready for an institution. Previously unreachable, T.J. gradually opened up to his family, finally learning to communicate in a whole new way. It was an awakening for them all.

Two years later, T.J.'s former third grade teacher saw him out on his bike, and they stopped to converse. She was so amazed at the change in him that she telephoned Becki immediately. Here was the child she remembered as uncommunicative and combative, looking bright-eyed, cheerful, and clear.

March of that same year brought a move to Montana for the Lindermans. This was a fresh start for T.J. He entered a new school, leaving behind his prior history, and found teachers who expected him to succeed. It was the first time in four years that T.J. was required to engage in regular classroom activities and to work at his appropriate grade level.

*   *   *

The Spring concert loomed ahead, and Becki awaited the day with trepidation. Would T.J. join in? Or would he stare blankly out at the audience and do nothing?

As luck would have it, T.J. was placed in the first row of children, just in front of the stage lights. Becki sat on the edge of her seat expectantly. She held her breath as T.J. first stared fixedly into the lights and then lifted his head to gaze out at the audience. The children began to sing while T.J. blinked his eyes and stared straight ahead. Slowly, he remembered the words and was soon joining in with the others. He didn't fall off the stage, and he completed the entire performance with only a few additional blinking episodes. Becki was ecstatic! She breathed a sigh of relief and marveled at how far they all had come.

T.J. Sonner is now an eighth grader in Darby, Montana. Though he is still a "nonstop explorer" and will always "dance to his own tune," his unique talents and charming nature continue to unfold. T.J. and his sister are building a healthy and harmonious relationship, and Becki feels that they now interact better than most siblings she knows. Brandee also eats the algae. She comments to her mother that when T.J. does slip into his old ways, she handles the conflict more calmly. Their whole family eats Super Blue Green Algae daily. They feel it has contributed immeasurably to their physical and mental health.

"I can't begin to explain how our lives have changed. We feel completely connected to the Cell Tech goals and vision. I have a deep gratitude to my Cell Tech family. Without the algae and the courage it took to make a change, I would not have my family as I now know it. I would not be looking into T.J.'s eyes and seeing the amazing sparkle of life that I now see every time I look at him. I have my son back."

Becki Linderman
Darby, Montana

"Angel"

"Not too long ago I was fortunate enough to receive an incredibly rewarding challenge," says Amy Phillips. "Friends of mine, parents of a special needs baby girl, had an opportunity to join a climbing expedition and they asked us to take care of their little one. Their older daughter would stay with Grandma. Mom and Dad had not been alone together since two year old Angel was born.

"Before our friends left on their vacation, my husband and I had been working with them to modify their baby's diet in an effort to improve her condition. Angel had been abusing herself by hitting her chin, her face, and her constantly infected ears. Her sleep was always fitful and troubled, and she frequently awakened tearfully. Her mother would cringe in bed with pillows over her ears to muffle the sound of her baby screaming. This often continued for hours at a time, leaving the whole family irritable and exhausted. When Angel was awake, she often appeared vacant and listless — off in her own small world. Many times, she was totally unreachable and unresponsive.

> *"To believe in angels is to believe in miracles. To believe in miracles is to know algae."*

"For several weeks, the baby's parents had been giving her Super Blue Green Acidophilus* and Super Blue Green Enzymes, noting small, gradual changes in her behavior. They suggested that we begin adding algae to her diet during their absence. In addition, Angel's doctor advised her mother to slowly reduce her daughter's medication. She asked us to continue this while they were gone. My husband and I were up to the challenge, and we approached our task enthusiasti-

* See page 175 for more information on Super Blue Green Acidophilus.

cally.

"While Angel's parents were away on their two-week vacation, we fed her Omega and Alpha Sun, Super Blue Green Acidophilus, and Super Blue Green Enzymes. Her improvement was astonishing! Progress came so rapidly that her condition seemed to change hourly. Amazingly, she began to smile, laugh, gurgle, reach, grab, hug, babble, make eye contact, and even sit up independently! This precious child no longer hit herself constantly, and her bruised hands and face began to improve.

"One day, in a restaurant, Angel grabbed a spoon and angrily began to beat the table. Previously, she would have remained distant and uncommunicative. Here she was having a normal, two year old tantrum! While most adults would welcome docile behavior, we cheered on our Terrible Two. This was the first time she had reacted to her environment in such a way."

*   *   *

These days, Angel has progressed even further — from tantrums to contentment. Her mother says that now, instead of Angel lying on the floor yelling and screaming (with rare moments of quiet contentment), she now smiles more frequently and seems calmer. Because she is also more responsive, she is more fun to be with.

Her previously distraught mother used to wonder what she could do to make her child happy. *What am I doing wrong?* she'd ask herself. The constant negative feedback was almost more than she could bear.

Now, although Angel still fusses occasionally during the night, she usually drops off to sleep quickly again on her own. Instead of enduring hours of agonizing screams, her grateful mother awakens alert and refreshed from a good night's rest.

Unfortunately, the strain of caring for a high-needs infant has stressed her parents' marriage to the breaking point. Amy has taken Angel into her home temporarily to ease the burden on her family.

"Recently, this angel baby came to be with me on a full-time basis," explains Amy. "We watch her improve everyday and rejoice in each miraculous moment. Holding this precious child's face in my hands, with her beautiful blond curly hair swirling around my fingers, looking deeply into her gorgeous blue eyes, I have seen true joy in her face and love in her heart. It is almost more than I can bear. I know that if she could talk, I would hear her sweet tiny voice whisper in my ear, 'Thank you.'"

Amy Phillips
Flagstaff, Arizona

Ian Frauts

Ian Frauts is twelve years old and in the seventh grade. One morning he ate two Omega Sun tablets with his breakfast and dashed off for school. At the end of the day, the door burst open as Ian rushed into the kitchen demanding "more of that stuff."

Ian Frauts

"What stuff?" asked his mother.

"You know, that B.G. stuff!" he exclaimed.

"Oh, the algae. What happened at school to make you feel this way?" she wondered aloud.

Ian explained that while he was sitting in math class, "All of a sudden, my brain went *pow, pow, pow* and I got all my math correct. I even beat the teacher!"

Up to this point, this child had struggled with his arithmetic. The concepts had often frustrated him, and he carried a 60% to 70% average. As a teacher herself, Amelia was often puzzled by Ian's difficulty. He had plenty of help at home, a good teacher at school, and a bright mind. Their family ate a nutritious diet and they were all health-oriented. Something must have been missing. . . .

Ian now eats his algae every day and keeps his math grades above 80%.

Tim Frauts, DDS and Amelia Frauts
Ontario, Canada

Daniel Jauregui

Dark-haired, dark-eyed Daniel wants to be an actor. Out going and fun-loving, he delights in making up his own jokes and creating off-the-wall sayings. He revels in the attention that drama brings and enjoys being in the limelight. "Everyone who meets him falls in love with him," says his mother proudly. "Even if I do say so myself!" When he is not acting, Daniel's surplus energy finds an outlet in after-school sports, especially soccer.

There was a time when Daniel's excess vitality boiled uncontrollably to the surface and erupted in nervous wiggling. First he shook his legs, then his hands. He just couldn't sit still! Instead of drifting easily off to sleep, he would toss and turn, unable to quiet his active mind or his fidgety body.

Daniel's teacher telephoned his mother regularly to complain about her son's inability to concentrate and focus in school. Though he often did well on exams, he rarely had the stamina to finish his daily assignments. When his concerned mother questioned him about it, Daniel exploded in frustration, "I can't help it. I don't *know* why!"

Unable to anticipate the consequences of his actions, Daniel sometimes lashed out at other children or broke objects impulsively. "Why did you do that?" his exasperated mother would ask.

"I don't know," he would reply mournfully. Daniel was always truly sorry for what he had done. He wanted to behave, but didn't have the self-control.

Dalene struggled with her options. She opposed medication, so she looked to his diet for answers. As an experiment, she decided to try giving him Super Blue Green Algae. It had "made a world of difference" for her, so perhaps Daniel would also benefit. She gave him one Alpha Sun on a Saturday morning, and continued this routine every day.

On Wednesday afternoon, Dalene drove to Daniel's school to pick him up and found a jubilant child waiting for her. He

Would you like to receive our catalog? Ransom Hill Press carries:

- Blue-Green Algae Related Books and Audios
- Multilevel/Network Marketing Books and Audios
- An exclusive collection of beautifully designed business-building postcards, t-shirts, and gift items

Ransom Hill Press
1-800-423-0620

Please call our 800 number to request a free catalog.
Or, tear out and mail the reply card below.

Please mail me your catalog.

I will also receive FREE the "Dear Venus" column for one year.
An exclusive from Ransom Hill Press.

Name: _____

Address: _____

City: _____ State: _____ Zip: _____

What MLM company are you with? _____

Comments: _____

Please mail my friend a catalog too.

Name: _____

Address: _____

City: _____ State: _____ Zip: _____

What MLM company are you with? _____

Comments: _____

BUSINESS REPLY MAIL
FIRST-CLASS MAIL   PERMIT NO. 361   RAMONA CA

POSTAGE WILL BE PAID BY ADDRESSEE

RANSOM HILL PRESS
PO BOX 325
RAMONA CA 92065-9932

IlIuIIIIIIuuIIuuIIIIIIuIIIuuIIuuIIIII

had completed all his work for the first time ever! Once more, the telephone rang with Daniel's teacher on the line. This time, however, instead of complaining about Daniel's poor performance, she questioned Dalene incredulously, "What happened to D.J.? He's a completely different child!"

Dalene also perceived an immediate change in her energetic son. Although he still has plenty of get-up-and-go, he can now sit still long enough to do his homework or watch a television program. His increased clarity seems to enhance his understanding of cause and effect. For example, in the past, if his sister hit him on the head accidentally with her ball, he would have chased her until he could hit her back. Now, he lets opportunities for retribution pass.

Recently, Daniel's school principal complimented him on not reacting aggressively to another child's bullying. Daniel controlled his anger and his response. His impulsive behavior has mellowed considerably.

"I'm a little concerned that Daniel's improvement has plateaued, though," comments Dalene. "I've noticed him slipping a little at school and at home." She plans to increase the amount of algae she is giving him to see if he is ready for more. She may add the Omega Sun, too. (Presently, he eats two Alpha Sun daily.)

Mrs. Jauregui notices in retrospect that Daniel and his teacher may have had difficulties in their relationship that contributed to his trouble in the classroom. But eating the algae helped him cope with that, too. According to Daniel's pediatrician, some of his behavior problems may stem from his having unusually high intelligence. He thinks this bright and gifted child may not be challenged enough in school.

This Christmas, Daniel will star in a Yuletide drama at their local church. Someday, this quick-witted, algae-eating thespian may appear on Broadway, or in a theater near you. Of course, his mother *knows* he's destined for greatness.

Dalene Jauregui
Ramona, California

Jeff R.

Jeff's birth mother was an alcoholic and unable to raise her son. She released him to a temporary foster home shortly after he was born. Here he felt loved, appreciated, and happy. At seven months of age, he was permanently adopted by another caring family. The parents both loved him as if he were their own. Eight months later, a little girl came to join them and their family was complete.

Jeff rarely cried, napped twice a day, and other parents remarked at how fortunate they were to have such a quiet baby. But when he grew to school age and began kindergarten, this taciturn child developed a stubborn, non-compliant streak. If the children were asked to participate in a group project, Jeff would sit resolutely in his chair with his arms crossed and refuse to join in. "I'm not interested in looking like the rest of those turkeys!" he would exclaim. One day, out of frustration, his teacher picked him up out of his chair with his body still in the sitting position and brought him over to the others.

From the beginning, learning came slowly for Jeff. When he was in the second grade, his mother realized that he was not reading the words but guessing at the answers. At this point, she became very active in his class by reading aloud to the children and closely monitoring Jeff's progress. Always a dreamer, he acquired the nickname "slowpoke," and because of a mild spasticity in his hands and feet, he appeared to be clumsy. "You know those springs in my hands," he once remarked to his mother, "they just knocked a pizza on the floor in the kitchen."

In fourth grade, a neurological evaluation delineated marked learning impairments. This translated into an inability to handle more than one instruction at a time. For instance, his mother could not ask him to clean his room. The enormity of the assignment would overwhelm him. She *could* request him, however, to pick up his socks, and when that job was complete, direct him to the next task.

When Jeff was in the fifth grade, the family had a visitor for their evening meal. This person recounted a disturbing story about a mutual friend of theirs whose teenager had attempted suicide. "Oh I think about that all the time," confessed Jeff airily. Later on that night when their children had gone to bed, his shocked parents discussed this horrifying outburst. They wondered if on some level, Jeff had always resented being taken from the home he had lived in as an infant. Perhaps this was why he wanted to die. How guilty and sad they felt! Determined to provide help for their troubled child, Jeff's parents took him to see a family counselor, who sent him to a psychiatrist. This doctor prescribed a mood elevating drug, which did offer some help. Jeff seemed a little more positive and could focus better, but was still very disorganized. Six months later, he received an additional prescription for antihistamines to cause drowsiness so that he could sleep.

Though Jeff's medication resulted in less negativity, he still exhibited episodes of uncontrolled anger by shouting loudly and clenching his fists. He bickered constantly with his little sister, accusing her of irritating him on purpose. "Shut up!" he would demand. Or, "Stop it! You're bothering me!"

Nutritionally, Jeff preferred anything white: white flour, white sugar, white rice, mashed potatoes, and macaroni — all refined carbohydrates. Once or twice a week, his mother would persuade him to choke down a few frozen peas or a couple of carrots. As he grew older, his mother found it even more difficult to influence his food choices, and in a busy family, her attention was often on other things.

Jeff's mother is an artist and a sculptress, and in September of 1995, a friend came to look at some of her artwork for sale. The last time they had seen this friend, she had been using crutches to walk. This day, Linda bounced into their home without assistance looking vibrant, healthy, and glowing. They were struck by her vitality. "What do you do in your life that gives you so much energy?" they asked. Linda told them about a wild-grown food with many vitamins and all the minerals and amino acids that the human body requires. Nutritionally complete, it had fed her body the elements she had been missing. She now felt better than she had in years.

Something had been absent from Jeff's diet for a long time, too, and his parents knew it. They had been looking for something to fill the gap, and they instinctively felt that Super Blue Green Algae would provide what he needed. Jeff began very simply by eating one Omega Sun and one Alpha Sun daily, and within four days, he showed a distinct change. He calmed down, focused better, and had more energy. After a week of eating algae, Jeff wasn't bickering with his sister and his attitude had improved. By the time a month had gone by, his teachers noticed that he seemed more compliant at school, and he smiled more often.

> *"Something had been absent from Jeff's diet for a long time..."*

Since early childhood, Jeff has been fascinated with all things military. War, guns, uniforms, and death captivated his imagination. A "gloom and doom" attitude seemed to accompany his fixation. After he began eating algae, his mood lightened, and military paraphernalia became less of an obsession. He developed more of a *can do* positivity, and he no longer dwells obsessively on suicide. Jeff's mother can even ask him to clean his room without being specific about each request, and he accomplishes the tasks without complaint. She doesn't think his new attitude has anything to do with his age, as the change came only after he began eating the algae.

At thirteen years old and 5'10" tall, Jeff is finally acquiring some control over his awkwardly large frame and uncooperative limbs. His mental outlook is healthier and his future seems bright. Jeff does remain on his mood elevating medication, but he now sleeps soundly without chemical inducement. At this time, Jeff eats two each of Alpha Sun and Omega Sun, and although he has only been eating Super Blue Green Algae for one year, his potential for well-being is limitless.

The family prefers to remain anonymous.

"Andy"

"Hi! My name is Andy. I am still in my mother's womb, but somehow I know that something is wrong with me. It could be caused by some strange chemicals that I've been subjected to since my conception. You see, my mother abused drugs and alcohol before and during her pregnancy. My father did, too.

"My birth is very difficult. I am premature, and I am very tiny — barely four pounds. In addition to that, my little body is not normal. It takes the doctors a while to discover what is wrong with me, but finally they give my condition a name. I can't remember the name, but there is supposed to be only about forty other kids alive that were born with the same problems. It is some kind of rare genetic thing. Yuk!

"My head, face, and jaws are badly deformed. I have only one ear, and I can't even hear out of that one. I can't cry, because I don't have any vocal chords. My lungs keep filling up with fluid and I have a terrible time breathing. I'm on the respirator so much that the doctors cut a hole in my throat and put in something they call a trache tube.

"Because I can't eat the way most normal babies do, the doctors make another hole in me that goes right into my stomach. That way, I can be fed through a tube. If that isn't bad enough, I can't move. I should be able to, but I can't! It's as if I have barely enough energy to stay alive. I need a miracle, and fast! I sure hope these doctors can come up with something to help me."

*   *   *

"I've been alive a few months now. I'm off the respirator a lot but the trache tube is still there. When I'm not on the machine, they have to pound me on the back six or seven times a day to knock the fluid out of my lungs. When it gets real bad, I'm back on the respirator again. They feed me through a tube with some kind of liquid stuff that comes out of a can. They can't put much in my tummy at a time, and I'm not growing as fast as I should. I still can't move. I am African-American, but I look so pale, you can hardly tell. I think my mother cares about me, but there is nothing she can do.

"Finally, I am leaving the hospital. Yippee! They are sending me to a foster home, where a lady is supposed to know how to care for kids like me. I can hardly wait!

"I think I am going to like this new arrangement better. This lady really cares for me. She talks to me a lot. I wish I could answer her or even just make a sound to let her know that I love her and appreciate what she is trying to do for me. We live on a little farm with a helipad next to it. A helicopter can land there to take me to a special hospital whenever my lungs get too congested.

"I am still very tiny. I weigh only five pounds, and I still can't move. This lady seems to love me; she must be an angel! I feel loved for the first time in my life. She changes my diapers, beats me on the back six times a day, and feeds me this liquid stuff through the feeding tube. I am not the only child with terrible problems whom she takes care of. She loves us all. My birth mother has finally given up on me. I can't blame her though — she's still my mother.

"My new foster mom is now adding something to that canned stuff. She is liquefying soft fruits and vegetables so she can pump that into my stomach, too. She also mixes some kind of green powder in with it. It's a good source of vitamins and minerals from barley leaves that helped some of the other kids.

"I really like being in this wonderful home, but I still can't move or even make a sound. Sometimes my lungs get so bad that they have to send the helicopter for me. It takes me back to that big old hospital where they put me on that machine again. I'm seventeen months old now, and I've been back there many times. Once, I was there for thirty-two days. They said that I died twice. My new mom and a paramedic both saved my life with CPR. Going to the hospital helps me get better so I can return home. That makes me glad."

*   *   *

"Today, my foster mom goes to visit an old friend. He is the nutritionist who told her about that green powder that she likes so much. He tells her about another green food that he thinks is a whole lot better. It helps the bodies of humans and animals to naturally take care of themselves better than anything he has ever heard of. It is called Super Blue Green Algae.

"Well, what happens after that seems almost like a miracle. She eats some of the algae stuff and in just one day, she feels much better. Mostly, she says that she has more energy than ever before. Wow! I need energy badly! The next day, she gives some to her husband (I love him, too) and he also feels some wonderful help right away. I sure hope she lets me eat some of that new stuff!

> *"What happens after that seems almost like a miracle."*

"The next day, when my mother fixes my meal, she puts just one capsule of Omega Sun algae powder in with the other things that she syringes into my little body. (I'm still only seven or eight pounds.) She continues to do this every meal. And, do you know what? I can tell the difference immediately. The next day, I don't have as much congestion in my lungs. They don't have to pound me on the back so much. I like that! I can't explain it, but some things are happening to me that have never happened before.

"I'm about eighteen months old now, and after just one or two weeks, I move for the first time. I do it all by myself. That is one of the most awesome moments in my short life! I have hope now! My lungs clear up so much that the helicopter never has to come back to the house any more. As time passes, all kinds of wonderful things begin happening to me. That algae stuff must really help the body help itself, just like my mom's nutritionist friend says it does."

*   *   *

"Well, eleven more months have passed now and my foster mom decides to take me to meet her special friend. She has never told him anything about me. I'm now able to sit up, I'm trying to stand, my skin color is normal, and I can play with all the other kids. I love playing with them, and they love playing with me. Everybody thinks I'm a little character! When mom's friend sees me for the first time and hears all about what has happened to me, tears appear in his eyes. I can tell he really likes helping people become healthy. He says that this is the very reason he became a nutritionist. Well, I'm certainly a lot healthier because he told my mom about this algae stuff. I love him, too."

*   *   *

"I will be three years old next month. Some really neat things have happened. After I stood up, I learned to walk. Now I can run! I can even run faster than my mom! I can fly up and down stairs like any normal child and I can open any door in the house. My mom thinks I'm a little rascal. She also thinks I'm a real bright boy, too. I know how to use all the buttons on the TV channel-changer. My foster dad can't even do that. Real soon, I am going to go to school. The teachers will show me how to use sign language. Wow! Life sure is exciting! I wonder what great thing is going to happen next?

"Think about it. Just eighteen months ago, I had never moved. I've come a long way, don't you think? I feel special. My foster mom and dad think so. I'm looking forward to the future and there is no telling what I'll be able to do. By the way, I am almost three feet tall and weigh about thirty-two pounds. You ought to see my muscles!

"I think I am normal. I think I can do anything. My parents feel the same way. I wish everybody would think so. My head is still deformed, and I still breathe and eat through tubes. I can grunt now, but I still can't talk, and I guess it will always be a little unusual to see someone with just one ear.

"Who knows? Maybe some day I'll be able to breathe without that hole in my throat, and my ear might even work. Perhaps I'll be able to talk so I can tell my parents and their friend that I love them. I can hardly wait to eat like a normal person so I can find out just what food tastes like — especially that Super Blue Green Algae stuff!"

Phil Haselden, DC
Kissimmee, Florida

Jeff Boyd

Lisa is a single mother of a very active, very rambunctious nine year old boy. Jeff has always been a high-needs child; even when he was a baby, he hardly slept. If Jeff didn't get his way, he would lie on the floor, kick his feet, and scream with rage. Sometimes he would stomp upstairs, slam his bedroom door, and then scream. His mother was afraid to take him anywhere with her because of his unruly behavior and "bad attitude." Now that Jeff was in school, his temper tantrums and angry outbursts spilled over into the classroom.

His short attention span and inability to focus prevented him from learning to read. School work became frustrating. One day, Jeff grew so agitated about something that he stomped his feet and ran from the classroom. The staff psychologist in Jeff's elementary school tested him for focus and concentration problems and assigned him to a special classroom for learning challenged children. When Lisa and Jeff moved to Mesa, Arizona, Jeff's behavioral problems continued, so his mother asked for him to be placed with other difficult students in his new school as well.

Unfortunately, his behavior deteriorated even further. He became so uncontrollable that his grandparents from California decided to remedy the situation. Grandpa Gabe has been the boy's only male role model, because Jeff's own father departed when his infant son was less than two months old. It was time for Grandpa to step in. Armed with a good supply of Super Blue Green Algae, Gabe and his wife Jill decided to spend the winter in Mesa.

First, they introduced the young troublemaker to Super Blue Green Algae. Then Grandpa Gabe religiously telephoned his grandson every evening after school to see how his day went. If it had been a difficult one, Gabe reassured him, "Today was a bad day. Tomorrow will be better." The next morning, he would call him again. "Today will be a wonderful day. You'll see."

Slowly, Jeff began to calm down. He became more compliant and less willful. Over the Christmas holiday, Jeff was out of school for one week, which he spent with his grandparents. As a single mother, Lisa worked ten hours a day with little time to manage her challenging youngster. With concentrated attention and consistent consumption of the algae, Jeff responded even better. Within three weeks, he began completing his school work, willingly accomplished his chores, and even took a shower without being asked. Incredible! One day, he brought a book into the living room where Lisa sat on the couch. With no prompting on her part, he confidently read the story to his shocked mother.

To everyone's amazement, within three months this bright, befreckled boy with a shock of sandy hair and a twinkle in his eye, entered and won his school math contest. Previously, he couldn't focus and concentrate well enough to complete his schoolwork, and his grades showed it. Here he was, representing his school and his family, and they were so proud!

Gabe thought Jeff should take a week's break from eating algae to see if he would assume his old patterns. Jill and Lisa refused. They quite liked the new Jeff, and weren't about to welcome the difficult one back! Lisa notices a perceptible difference in her son's demeanor if he doesn't eat his algae for a few days. They "have little battles over everything," and she'll "have to tell him to do something a thousand times." She says that Jeff is much more fun to be around now, and she misses him when he's gone instead of wishing he would go!

Jeff even feels a difference in his body. "At recess, I can run better, faster, and farther. I can breathe better because my nose isn't stuffed up."

Now, at ten years old, Jeff has become a champion motorcross bicycle racer. He began as a novice, where he quickly won six first place awards. He then moved up to the intermediate level, and out of two races there, Jeff has had two second place finishes. All this from a little boy who used to peddle his bicycle aimlessly about the track with no goal and no motivation. Just prior to moving up to intermediate, Jeff competed with two thousand other children from all around the country in the largest race in Arizona, The Winter Nationals in Phoenix. In the novice class for his age group, Jeff took home the first place trophy — one that stands almost as tall as he does!

Although Jeff's grandparents have moved from Mesa to Sedona, they keep a close eye on their bright, blossoming, bicycle-riding grandson. Because of the algae, introduced to him by his Grandpa Gabe, Jeff has begun to take the high road to achievement, activity, and accomplishment. He even likes his algae so much that he questions his mother, "Mom! Have you had your algae today?"

Instead of driving people away with his disruptive, unfocused behavior, this well-mannered young man is often praised by his friends' parents. "You know what. . ." they say, "that child is welcome here anytime!" Music to any mother's ears.

Gabe Dick
Sedona, Arizona

2

Adult Stories

A Smile is a Blessing

You ask me why I wear a smile?
I am happy, I am healthy, I have fun;
I am thankful, I am wealthy, I have love;
I am balanced, I am wise, I have joy.
My body moves with ease and grace;
My mind is sharp and clear.
I am at peace with myself and all I connect with;
My heart is joyful as I breathe so deeply.
I am a blessing to those I touch;
And I am blessed by those who touch me.
And you ask me why I wear a smile?

Esther Michel
Auburn, California

Linda Oyama

At the age of forty-seven, Linda Oyama found herself suffering from the effects of two debilitating medical conditions: one interfered with heart function, and the other caused her to shuffle as she walked, when she could walk. Drooling and shaking, her posture became rigid and stooped. Eventually, she spent most of her time in a wheelchair. Linda's husband had to dress and feed her, as she could no longer lift her arms or walk without support.

Linda Oyama before eating Super Blue Green Algae.

Before this, Linda had been an active, vital, athletic woman. "Hunting, fishing, camping, running a trapline in winter months, skiing, snowshoeing, and horseback riding were but a few of the things that made my world go around," she recalls.

Dying slowly and deserted by the medical profession, Linda suddenly realized where the responsibility for her health lay. It struck her that she, not doctors, Medicaid, Medicare, or her health insurance was totally in charge of her situation. This knowledge galvanized her into searching for alternatives.

Along the way, Linda found many caring people to support her in choosing natural health care methods. One of Linda's friends told her about a wonderful superfood that might help her recover. According to Linda, "It proved to be one of the most powerful forces in bringing my health under control." She discontinued many of her other supplements and hasn't looked back since. Linda no longer sleeps fourteen hours each day, and she has returned to her hunting, fishing, and oil painting. Not only does she ride her horses and walk without assistance, she can run freely as well. With her thick curly hair flowing past her shoulders, and her broad sunshiny smile, Linda is a radiant picture of health. Although she admits to having a slight tremor when she is nervous, it is a pale remnant of the jellylike shaking she experienced during her illness. Lest she forget how far she has come, Linda leaves her own funeral instructions — the written arrangements she had drawn up when her life had seemed to be coming to an

*Linda Oyama on
the road back to health.*

end — by the telephone as a reminder of the tenuousness of life.

"Getting well and staying well begins with you. No one can do it for you. Taking care of your health is a lifelong commitment." From this transformational experience, Linda has gained a wealth of wisdom that she wishes to share with others. . . .

*Linda Oyama
Bozeman, Montana*

Katia Freedman

Katia Freedman came with her husband to the United States to make a new life. They had fled their homeland during Russia's persecuting pogroms against Jews after 1922. After an arduous trip over the European continent, they embarked on the long journey across the Atlantic ocean to their new home. Born in Crimea, in the former Soviet Union, this stalwart woman with a Russian work ethic became the matriarch of a large, closely knit family.

The Freedmans struggled to survive in a new country with unfamiliar customs and a strange sounding language. Previously an actress, Katia took up sewing and became a masterful seamstress. As her family grew, she spent many long hours at the sewing machine, skillfully fashioning tailored coats and jackets for her husband and grandsons. Her hands fairly flew as she magically created extraordinarily stylish gowns for her beautiful daughters.

Her progeny adored her. Katia often spun tales of life in the old country and the travails of living in a strange, new land. To her grandsons Steven and Robert, their fascinating grandmother took on mythic proportions as the living record of their family history.

When she fell and broke her hip at the advanced age of ninety-one, Katia lost her independence, her stamina, and her strength. Her family watched helplessly as she first deteriorated physically, then mentally. Confined to her bed in a rest home, and weighing only 80 pounds, Katia's view of the future looked bleak. Depressed about her dwindling capacities, she would pray to be released from her body. She often lamented tearfully to her grandson, "Oh, Steven, I just want to *die*."

"But, Grandma," he would reply, "if you were dead, then we wouldn't be visiting!" How sad the frail shell of a woman lying in the bed in front of him made him feel!

Katia refused the recommended physical therapy exercises, and her muscles began to atrophy. Her sarcastic wit and the twinkle in her eye disappeared. Most frustrating of all, her mental acuity began to fail. Many times she wouldn't recognize her own daughter, Steven's mother, Anita, even though she spent several hours with her daily.

Years later, after Robert and Steven each had a positive experience eating Super Blue Green Algae, they suggested giving it to their bedridden grandmother. Because Steven's mother had the best opportunity to visit the family matriarch, she volunteered for the assignment. Every day, Anita mixed the green powder into a glass of prune juice or other fruit drink, and gave it to her frail mother. She didn't tell her what she was drinking because she likely wouldn't understand or care. Nevertheless, the green ring around her mouth gave her away!

The most remarkable change for this nonagenarian came almost immediately after starting on the Spectrabiotics. The improvement in her intestinal flora decreased her digestive irregularity, which apparently astounded her doctors. (As Steve says, a ninety-seven year old without constipation is a miracle, indeed!)

After Katia had been drinking her algae every day for four months, Steve's mother called him to indicate that Grandma's customary sarcastic wit had reappeared. Apparently, a doctor had entered her room to inquire after her health as he often did, but this time she responded to his *How are you?* by retorting, "I don't know. You're the doctor, you tell me!"

No longer fading quietly away in her hospital bed, Katia Freedman regained her positive outlook on life. She reminisced with her family, recalling many fond memories and recognizing everyone who came to visit. This Russian-born *babushka* with little muscle tone and no ability to move on her own began to rebuild her slight frame and reconstruct her mental clarity. She consumed acidophilus, bifidus*, enzymes, Alpha Sun, and Omega Sun regularly.

---

* See page 175 for more information on Super Blue Green Bifidus.

One day when Steven came to visit, instead of begging to die, she raised her gnarled, bony hand "riddled with arthritis" and sighed in frustration. No longer able to sew a fine seam or skillfully hem a gown, this contracted and deformed hand showed the passage of time and the gruelling effects of a hard life. "Look, Steven!" she complained. "I'm no good. I can't do what I used to do."

"Grandma," he answered, "we're talking, and that's something!"

"Yes," she admitted. "It's so nice to be with you."

Sad though this exchange was, Steven appreciated every precious moment he had with his special Grandma. She passed away gently this year on July 2nd. While the extra mental clarity she had up until the moment of her death might seem like a small gain to some, Steven and his family only felt the joy of conversing with Katia and having her recognize and remember them all. Instead of slipping away behind a veil of mental fog and lost memories, Katia Freedman spent many happy moments reminiscing with her descendents. At the time of her passing, this resilient Russian immigrant had nearly reached her ninety-eighth birthday.

With the combination of a wild grown food and balanced digestive aids, the quality and quantity of the twilight years can be greatly enhanced. In Katia's case, it allowed her and her family many more precious memories to add to the family album.

Steven Kasower
Sacramento, California

Ann Taylor, PT

Ann Taylor ("Taylor") lived and worked in Burlington, Vermont. She maintained a private practice in Sports Medicine, Orthopedics, and Physical Therapy. Seven years ago, she met a fellow professional, Iginia Boccalandro, a bodyworker who specialized in Rolfing. The two entrepreneurial women quickly developed a professional and personal relationship based on friendship and trust.

Approximately a year later, Iginia introduced her friend to Super Blue Green Algae. Sceptical of this simple food, Taylor sporadically ingested a few capsules and then returned it, complaining that it "didn't work."

For the next five weeks, Iginia vigilantly watched her friend to ensure her regular intake of the algae. "After that time, I started to miss it when I didn't eat it," Taylor admits. "I woke up more easily and felt more alive throughout my day." As a self-described "cutting-edge" physical therapist interested in alternative medicine, she included nutritional counselling in her practice. Her clinic employed a full-time nutritionist to teach clients about the relationship between diet and health. Algae smoothies were available as a refreshment following therapy sessions.

After Taylor had eaten algae herself for three months, she noticed a reduction in symptoms surrounding her menstrual cycle. Athletic improvement followed: Her stamina increased while skiing long hours on her days off. She and Iginia moved to the bottom of Little Cottonwood Canyon, in Utah to follow their passion for the slopes. Known as the "Powder Queen of Snowbird," Taylor became famous for her blue-green teeth. All smiles after "successful powder runs," she would board the tram and eagerly chat with the other riders. Invariably, multiple BG Bites* would have temporarily left their mark on her pearly whites!

* For more information on BG Bites, please see page 176.

*   *   *

Every year in August, Iginia and Taylor made the annual pilgrimage to Klamath Falls for Cell Tech's week-long celebration. Each time they flew over Mount Shasta, in northern California, they wondered at its mystique and beauty. It called to them, until they finally decided to climb to its peak.

They found themselves at the 8,000 foot base camp of the mountain, gazing up at the perpetual ring of clouds around its summit. The day before, they had rented all the equipment they thought they would need, including crampons (spiked metal shoes) and ice axes. Neither of them realized that the route they would travel required *medium* mountaineering skills. Woefully unprepared, but in blissful ignorance, they set off. It was 4:30 a.m.

The caretaker at the Sierra Club hut recommended the *couloir*, or red chimney, as the best way to climb to the top of her majesty. It turned out to be a steep gutter of ice, much longer than Taylor had imagined it would be. Kicking the toe of her crampon into the hard, icy walls and then hacking a handhold with the axe, she struggled slowly up the incline with Iginia leading the way. At one point, perspiring with fear and exhaustion, Taylor called out to her companion for support and guidance, "Iginia...." Tears streamed down her face and she sobbed in frustration. It was taking so long. Would they ever make it to the top? Iginia in turn looked down at her faltering friend and realized, "Oh, my God! If I do anything wrong, I'll fall and kill her!" They persevered up the four hundred foot chimney until they collapsed in a heap at the top. But they weren't done yet. There were snow fields to cross, a false summit to reach, glaciers to negotiate, and Misery Hill to ascend.

When the two intrepid mountaineers finally reached the top of the volcanic peak nine hours later, they gazed out at the crystal blue sky to the vast expanse below. Look how far they had come! The highest Taylor had ever climbed before had been 11,000 feet. This was a gruelling 3,200 feet higher. "Yeah! I did it!" she screamed.

The return trip involved "glissading" down vertical snow fields on their buttocks using their axes as brakes and making long treks in the blinding sun over glaciers of ice. Dehydrated and affected by the extreme altitude, Taylor rested in the shade of a tree on the way down. Five hours later, they finally returned to the bottom of the challenging mountain. The entire trip had taken fourteen and a half hours.

Taylor tripled her algae intake before her climbing expedition and feasted on BG Bites throughout her day. That evening, she also downed extra Super Sprouts & Algae* and rehydrated herself with clean, fresh water. Although she felt tired and depleted the next day, she was amazed that she had no muscle soreness. Taylor feels that Super Blue Green Algae is an "extraordinary food for high alpine activities such as mountaineering, mountain biking, skiing, and hiking." Super Sprouts & Algae, especially, seems to help flush the lactic acid from sore muscles.

Ann Taylor (left), shortly after medical treatment, with Alice Colwell eating fresh blue-green algae out of Klamath Lake.

*　　　　*　　　　*

Several years later, Ann Taylor received the news that she had a life-threatening illness. She describes herself as "a driven, type-A personality who never rested and worked hard." Typical to her Virgo birth sign, she worried constantly and often immersed herself in negative thoughts and attitudes. She feels these characteristics may have predisposed her to the devel-

* See page 176 for more information on Super Sprouts & Algae.

opment of a breast condition that struck fear in her heart.

The path before her was unclear. Although steeped in traditional Western thought regarding sickness and disease, she felt strongly that natural methods had something to offer. However, her medical friends quoted statistics and admonished her against seeking alternative therapies. She investigated all the possibilities open to her and chose a blending of both disciplines.

Taylor entered the local hospital for surgery. All went well and the doctors released her the following day to recover at home. She chose a follow-up program of medical care and medication. Three weeks later, she traveled to the Hippocrates Health Clinic in Florida where she immediately began a cleansing program to strengthen and detoxify. Here, she "learned remarkable things, and met a lot of wonderful people," many of whom recommended Super Blue Green Algae. Even the director of the clinic suggested its inclusion in her diet.

Soon after returning from the clinic, she began a six month program of medication that usually results in weakness and exhaustion. Marta Kollman, cofounder of Cell Tech, came to her assistance by sending her care packages of Super Q_{10},* algae, and Sprouts and Algae. Taylor and Marta had met during the first post-August Celebration† river rafting trip and had formed a quick bond. "Honey," Marta wrote, "we expect to be running rivers with you 'til we're all wearing dentures. Eat more algae!"

With the help of Super Blue Green Algae and the support of her Cell Tech friends, this "one-breasted, bald-headed Amazon woman" kept up a rigorous schedule of skiing and traveling, with strength and vitality to spare. Even though her medical treatment involved noxious chemicals, Taylor remained healthy by using wheat grass, Chinese herbs, and all the algae products Marta had so generously sent to her. Taylor also added a week of meditation at a health and yoga center, mind-

* See page 176 for more information on Super Q_{10}.
† The August Celebration is held at the beginning of August every year. It is a gathering of Cell Tech distributors, their families, and friends for the purpose of learning and sharing about Super Blue Green Algae.

fulness training, psychotherapy, group therapy, and prayer. She now has a head of brownish-gray, curly hair!

The high point along Taylor's journey was her first encounter with Daryl Kollman, also a cofounder of Cell Tech. "I've met many CEO's," she sighs, "but meeting Daryl was a life-altering experience. He took my hand in both of his and beamed his love at me. Wow! That was really special."

Ann Taylor sees herself as a "grandmother spirit" in Cell Tech. She has been eating algae for six years and teaching others about nutrition along the way. This blue-green miracle gave her the gift of life and the freedom to pursue her dreams.

Ann Taylor, PT
Salt Lake City, Utah and Lake Champlain, Vermont

Sandy Schultz, LPN

When Sandy Schultz reached mid-life she says her body "fell apart." During the winter in Wisconsin, when the windows and doors remained shut, the uncirculated air carried irritating dust mites that caused her eyes to water and her nose to run. The buildup of mucous in her lungs stimulated coughing episodes that brought a barrage of clear fluid from her lungs. A steroid inhaler dulled her discomfort, but the attacks never completely disappeared.

After dragging herself home from work as a practical nurse, Sandy would flop down on the couch where she remained until bedtime. Unfortunately, the intermittent coughing fits regularly interrupted her sleep, leaving her tired and listless throughout the day. Was she doomed to this vicious cycle for the rest of her life? Nothing she tried brought her any relief.

Just prior to attending her family reunion, Sandy received a tape in the mail that raved about the benefits of Super Blue Green Algae. To her, it sounded exceedingly outrageous, and she promptly forgot about it. It just so happens, however, that the people who sent Sandy the tape lived very near the reunion site, so she and her husband decided to visit them. During their stay, their hostess offered Sandy a "BG Bite, one Alpha Sun, and one Omega Sun." Although she felt uncomfortable about accepting something she knew little about, she trusted her friend and ate the algae with her breakfast.

By late afternoon, when Sandy would usually have experienced a slump, she felt as energetic as she had in the morning. "Could it be the algae?" she wondered. Her husband, a registered nurse, assured her that her results were probably psychological. Nevertheless, when Sandy returned home, she decided to try Alpha and Omega Sun. Her results speak for themselves.

Sandy ate her algae regularly and quickly experienced change. One busy week, after using her inhaler only sporadically, she noticed that her allergy symptoms had lessened. She had no more discharge from her eyes, nose, or lungs. The sceptical nurse in Sandy still couldn't accept that a simple food could alter her internal environment so significantly in such a short period of time. Three weeks went by, and then four. One morning, Sandy awoke with completely clear lungs and no wheezing. She was ecstatic!

Now when Sandy returns from a long day at work, she has ample energy to walk downstairs to the basement to do laundry or other household chores. With an uninterrupted night's sleep, she awakes fresh and ready for her day. In addition, she has renewed motivation to exercise regularly, which adds to her feeling of aliveness and joy. Sandy has no words to express her gratitude at the change in her health picture. Instead of being relegated to a life of coughing, wheezing, and low vitality, she's able to engage in activities that bring her optimism and hope. Even her doubting Thomas husband is eating algae and experiencing more vigor and energy.

Recently, Sandy sent her allergist the tape that sparked her interest, "Who Stole America's Health" by Dr. Erwin Gemmer. She plans to share Super Blue Green Algae with other members of the medical profession.

The personal exchange of hope, health, and freedom will not only alter our own lives, but the lives of others throughout the world.

Sandy Schultz, LPN
Greenfield, Wisconsin

Dorothy Zelle

Dorothy Zelle entered the emergency room with a rup-
tured fallopian tube. Her bloated abdomen throbbed unbear-
ably as she slipped in and out of consciousness.

The doctor was emphatic: immediate surgery. Dorothy
emerged from her fog long enough to refuse the possibility of
a blood transfusion during the operation. Even in her delirium,
she was concerned about possible negative side-effects of using someone else's blood. Once more, she faded away.

The surgery went well, though Dorothy lost nearly half
her blood volume. She recalls being aware of observing the
process from a vantage point high above the operating table.
Should she drift away completely, or should she return?

"We nearly lost you," said the doctor when Dorothy regained consciousness. "And because of the extensive hemor-
rhaging, you'll need a long time to recover." She estimated
that it might take four months before Dorothy would feel up
to resuming her job. This was impossible! As a self-employed
massage therapist and single mother, Dorothy could ill-afford
to take that much time off from work.

Prior to her surgery, Dorothy had been eating algae regularly, but with the doctor's grim prognosis, she consumed it
in earnest. She ate fifty to one hundred capsules each day,
and saw improvement immediately. (Super Blue Green Algae
is a superior source of chlorophyll, which is similar to hemoglobin, and Vitamin B12, which is important for the metabo-
lism of iron. Both are essential for building rich new blood.)

Dorothy's improvement was swift. To everyone's amazement, within three and a half weeks, this 5' 2", 110 pound
fighter returned to her massage practice full-time, gradually
increasing her client load until she was back to her previous
schedule.

Dorothy Zelle
Colfax, California

Bonnie Seltzer

Bonnie's twenty-eighth birthday dawned gloomy and cold, not outside her window, but inside her heart. For two weeks, strange and inexplicable symptoms had progressively warned her that all was not well. When she awakened on that fateful morning, her body would not respond to any of the messages her brain sent. "My neck refused to carry the weight of my head. My fragmented vision was coupled with my inability to direct my eyeballs, and when I spoke, I sounded like a stroke victim. Try as I might, the words would not come out without a great deal of hesitation."

As the morning progressed, Bonnie began to experience an electric sensation down her right arm, radiating into her hand, almost as if she had been plugged into an electric socket. She telephoned her medical doctor, frantically insisting that he see her before his first patient. After examining her, the doctor suggested that she might have what he referred to as a "pinched nerve." Because Bonnie had heard that Chiropractic care might help this type of condition, she made an appointment with her local chiropractor.

When she returned home after her chiropractic visit, Bonnie paced the floor agitatedly, unable to sit still for the next few hours. Every spot on her body ached, and her arms and legs moved independently of voluntary control. After spending a short time on the couch, she tried to walk to her bedroom. Suddenly, without warning, her legs locked, then buckled, and she sank to the floor, paralyzed.

Later that evening, after being carried to her bed, she found that she was unable to swallow any food. Even more frightening, she couldn't breathe!

She remembers thinking, "What an unusual sensation to try to inhale, but have the lungs not respond." The next few moments seemed surreal. From somewhere far away, a rosy, pink light invited her, called to her, beckoned her to come. Bonnie felt so tempted to follow, but something drew her back.

Suddenly, she was able to breathe again; it wasn't time to go.

The next day Bonnie could walk, but she had limited control of her limbs. With arms and legs "flying off in all directions," she entered a neurologist's office. He examined her and concluded that she seemed to be suffering from a particularly virulent strain of the flu which other people in her area had been experiencing. In his opinion, this virus had settled into her central nervous system. Bonnie desperately wanted to believe this diagnosis, but in her heart, she intuitively felt that her condition was not the flu, but a progressive neurological disorder that often reverses itself temporarily, only to reappear once again.

Within three weeks, she had almost returned to her old self. Two years later, however, medical tests finally confirmed Bonnie's previous fears. Her illness was indeed a well known but little understood disorder of the nervous system that is chronic and progressive. The ailment is characterized by the development of multiple lesions in the brain and spinal cord and the gradual destruction of myelin, a fatty substance that sheaths the nerve fibers. Just as stripping the insulation from electrical wires decreases their conductivity, a breakdown of the myelin sheath interferes with the ability of nerves to transmit messages between body and brain. This explains why Bonnie's body often did not respond to her conscious commands.

After she had a second attack of even more debilitating symptoms than she had initially endured, Bonnie's neurologist suggested that she learn to live with it. She'll never forget the day he made that statement to her on the phone. With tear-filled eyes, she gazed out the kitchen window at her daughter's sandbox. "Learn to live with it," she thought, as rivulets of tears cascaded down her face, "how can I do that?"

During the next four years, Bonnie remained housebound, and ultimately, bedridden. This gave her time to research her various treatment options and expand upon the changes she had made previously, which had included the elimination of sugar, white flour, and caffeine, the addition of high protein, low carbohydrate foods, and increased doses of vitamins and minerals.

At the time, megavitamin therapy was a popular remedy for illness and disease. While Bonnie initially responded quite well to this regimen, she quickly discovered that her body could no longer receive balanced, vitalistic nourishment from such a program. After severe allergies surfaced, she realized that this approach was not the answer.

Subsequently, Bonnie sampled a variety of therapies in this country and overseas, some traditional and some bizarre. One day, she became so frustrated that she refused to be poked, prodded, and experimented on any more. "My days of submission as a human guinea pig desperately seeking a cure came to a screeching halt. My clinical intellect lay in a heap on the floor in the midst of exquisite agony and suffering. I bottomed out."

At the deepest moment of her despair, Bonnie received two answers to her prayers for direction. Ironically, after travelling to far off treatment centers in Mexico and Germany, she discovered the first gift right in her own hometown of Brooklyn, New York: Dr. Donald Epstein, the founder and developer of a unique method of healing called Network Chiropractic.* This system relies on the premise that the body will heal itself as long as there is no interference to the free flow of nerve impulses from the brain and spinal cord to all parts of the body. Because her condition was neurologically based, Bonnie thought she might respond well to this approach. Through her chiropractic care with Dr. Epstein, Bonnie's nervous system began to become clearer and more alive. By her own admission, she finds it difficult to describe the transformative power of her experience with Network Chiropractic. Nevertheless, she experienced the change.

Bonnie also came in contact with Super Blue Green Algae. Her previous nutritional research supported the premise that a wild-grown food contains trace elements, vitamins, and minerals not found in synthetically produced supplements. She was anxious to see if the algae might provide her with some nutrients she was lacking. Initially, her results were disappoint-

---

* See page 180 for more information about Network Chiropractic.

ing, but realizing that her deficiencies were severe and long-standing, Bonnie decided to try adding even more algae to her daily intake. When she reached the magic number of twenty-four capsules a day, a large amount by anyone's standards, changes began to occur.

"It was as if my life suddenly lit up with light!" she relates. "Nothing [else] had ever generated such an impact on my energy, stamina, physical strength, mental clarity, and ability to cope with stress."

One morning, Bonnie awakened with such a newfound zest for life and optimistic attitude that she decided to walk the mile to work. Previously, she had required a ride to her part-time job. "My mother was

Bonnie Seltzer (looking fabulous!) is now exercising again and enjoying an active life.

concerned that my legs might suddenly buckle without warning, but I chose to listen to the reassuring voice within my own head telling me to go for it! I'll never forget that day. Tears of joy streamed down my face as I reached my destination. In the beginning, I wasn't consistently strong enough to walk the distance more than a few times per week, but it was definitely a turning point in my quest for health."

Recently, Bonnie Seltzer has regained enough flexibility in her body to return to yoga exercises. She can also walk very quickly, climb up and down stairs at a rapid pace, dance, and run for short distances. She has begun offering nutritional and wholistic health consultations for other people suffering from similar degenerative neurological conditions, describing herself as an "educator, lecturer, Nutrition Resource Consultant, and [Independent] Distributor of Super Blue Green Algae."

Bonnie consumes an enzymatically rich diet that balances proteins, carbohydrates, and fatty acids in a calculated ratio. Super Blue Green Algae is a "foundational food" making up a portion of her protein requirement in the form of amino acids.

This previously incapacitated woman, who remained confined to her bed for one year and house bound for five, never thought she'd have another life. "I feel reborn!" she exults.

Bonnie Seltzer
Brooklyn, New York

Cheryle Winn

Cheryle Winn consulted with an intuitive reader who provided her with the following poem.

> I am the lady of the lake;
> I am the spirit of water.
> I held your children
> And watched them grow.
> If you will once again
> Allow me to enter you,
> Together we will create
> The heaven on earth
> We know shall come.

Cheryle Winn
Medford, Oregon

Madalyn Suozzo

Madalyn's father called her with bad news: Doctors had discovered that he had a serious prostate condition for which they could offer little help. It had already spread to other parts of his body, including his spine.

Determined to help him, Madalyn flew from California to his bedside in New York and hired a macrobiotic cook to prepare his meals. During Madalyn's visit, the cook told them both about Super Blue Green Algae. They acquired an initial supply, consumed it, and then promptly forgot about it. Madalyn's concern for her father and their search for treatment eclipsed everything else.

Eighteen months later, Madalyn began experiencing her own physical problems. Her debilitating, chronic fatigue would not respond to conventional care, so she looked elsewhere. She remembered the algae she had eaten many months before, and felt intuitively that it would help her overcome her exhaustion. She began eating it regularly and consistently. Within three months, Madalyn's health turned completely around. Her energy and well-being were greater than ever before!

Conversely, Madalyn's father was not well. By the summer, he had dropped from 145 to 117 pounds because he was unable to keep his food down. He was also suffering from excruciating bone distress. She again flew to New York, thinking this would be the last time she would see her father alive.

When Madalyn entered the room where her father sat, she caught her breath. There sat a ghostly shadow of the robust, Italian patriarch who had raised four spirited children. He used to be so healthy. People often commented on how young he looked. In his place, slumped in the over-stuffed easy chair that had become his bed, sat a shrivelled, haggard, wisp of a man. Though Madalyn had already processed a great deal of grief over losing the father she had once known, she was unprepared for the extent of his deterioration.

Previously, Mr. Suozzo had owned his own plumbing supply warehouse and was well respected by his community and his church. Though not a big man or talkative, many people in his community looked up to him, and he loved his wife and children with a passion. Madalyn couldn't watch her father slip away from them now. He still had so much life to live.

Madalyn began working with her father using a special type of work that transfers electromagnetic energy through her hands to his body. The intent was to stimulate his cells to replace themselves in a healthy way, instead of growing wildly out of control. Because she had been teaching this method to others as well as using it on clients of her own, Madalyn was confident that she would see a change. Much to her surprise, her father trusted her completely and followed her recommendations conscientiously.

Knowing that he was unable to keep solid food in his stomach, and realizing the importance of good nutrition during the repair process, Madalyn thought about a liquid nourishment for him. Her solution was to add fifty capsules of algae each day to fresh juiced vegetables. A visit to an acupuncturist cleared up his sluggish digestive system, and because he was able to process and assimilate the drinks Madalyn prepared for him, he soon began to regain his strength and vitality. He also continued on his medication and physician-prescribed hormone shots.

After caring for her father for six weeks and watching a gradual and steady improvement in his condition, Madalyn looked at him one day in astonishment and blurted out, "Dad! You're not dead yet!"

"Yeaahh," he drawled, as if to ask, "what's your point?"

"If you pull through this," his stalwart daughter replied, "I'll pack up and move back to New York." And that's just what she did.

Mr. Suozzo and his wife celebrated their fiftieth wedding anniversary last year with much merry making and plenty of hope for the future. Shortly thereafter, however, Madalyn's father experienced a setback: While vacationing in Florida for the winter, his previous illness recurred. After undergoing radiation therapy, he weakened considerably. Fortunately, when he returned to New York, Madalyn began using her energy work and monitoring his algae intake again, and his health improved once more.

Today, Mr. Suozzo is not only up and out of his chair, but has returned to work with vigor. As of today, seven years after his initial illness, Madalyn's father is alive, alert, and flourishing.

Madalyn Suozzo
Saugerties, New York

Dr. Franklyn Cook, MD

A popular television doctor inspired young Franklyn Cook to enroll in medical school. As an obstetrician for thirty years, he helped people start their families by offering fertility guidance and delivering babies, a stressful but personally satisfying occupation.

Then one day, as Dr. Cook approached sixty years old, things changed. While relaxing after dinner with a cup of coffee, he coughed into his napkin and saw an ominous spot of blood. The next day, he consulted with a specialist who took a chest x-ray. Without delay, the good doctor found himself on someone else's operating table to have his right lung removed.

An unfortunate complication of the surgery resulted in damage to the nerves supplying his right vocal chord: Franklyn Cook could not talk. "Dear Lord," he silently prayed, "how can I help people if I can't talk?" It seems an angel was sent to answer his prayers. Some time after the operation, the Cooks went to dinner with some friends who, in turn, invited a mutual acquaintance to join them. Sue Conover, Frank's angel, walked into the restaurant looking slim, trim, and vibrantly healthy, wearing a button on her chest that said, "I eat algae. Ask me why."

Completely taken by her glowing appearance, the group naturally asked her, "What about algae?" Sue brought an audio tape to the Cooks' home, but it didn't take much convincing for Frank to catch on. Whatever Sue was doing, he wanted some of it!

This dyed-in-the-wool physician with classical medical schooling and no nutritional training found himself eating something he thought grew in swimming pools and fish tanks. Results came quickly, however. His energy level began to increase, and he became more focused and alert. At the same time, his nervous system became more balanced. One day, he lifted a jar of mayonnaise from the refrigerator and felt it slip out of his hands. It crashed to the tile floor and shattered. Mayonnaise and glass were everywhere. Frank didn't swear; Frank didn't shout. He calmly and quietly cleaned up the sticky mess and continued on. In the past, sparks would have flown, but this day, he remained centered and in control.

Today, Dr. Cook also notices that although he sleeps less hours, he sleeps more soundly. In the past, he would arise at five in the morning to let out his two meowing cats and then find himself unable to go back to bed. Now, he jumps up to release the complainers and then curls up for two more hours of restful slumber.

He accomplishes so much more because he has extra hours in the day, and his high energy level leads to greater productivity. Going from "a hundred mile an hour obstetrical practice to zero miles an hour" following his surgery was a difficult transition, mentally and physically. Because of his new commitment to

> *"Today, he exhibits no sign of his previous disability."*

helping others with Super Blue Green Algae, Frank Cook has a reason to get up in the morning. Everyday he asks himself, "What can I do to share this with people?" He loves the way he feels!

The most surprising and gratifying change in Frank Cook's experience came after he had been eating Super Blue Green Algae for about four months: his speech began to return. Today, he exhibits no sign of his previous disability. Thanks to his angel, Sue Conover, this sixty year old retired physician says he feels as well and healthy as a man half his age.

Recently, Dr. Cook made the commitment to accomplish Double Diamond level in the Cell Tech marketing plan by sharing Super Blue Green Algae with as many people as possible. His goal is to teach others, especially members of his own profession, that nutrition can prevent many debilitating illnesses. Though he has convinced three of his medical colleagues to begin eating the algae, he says many fellow doctors don't want to know about nutrition. He won't give up easily, however. Obviously, this man is a fighter, and if he says he'll do it, he will!

Dr. Franklyn Cook, MD
Carmichael, California

Postscript: As a side note, Frank's previously frail, seventy-four year old mother-in-law (who now eats algae), grabbed his hand to jitterbug with him before they exited the dance hall at a recent wedding reception!

Cindy Bertrand

Cindy Bertrand lives with her son, Jonathan, in a two-story house in Toronto, Canada, a bustling, metropolitan city of five million people. Once a struggling actress/waitress with an uncertain future, she now earns a substantial income through Cell Tech to support herself and her young son. More importantly, Cindy has acquired health and hope along the way.

Between the ages of twenty-one and twenty-seven, Cindy Bertrand struggled in the shadows of Hollywood, sporadically acting in television commercials and working as a waitress on the side to pay her bills. She reluctantly confesses to living "the fast life," dishonoring her body by staying up late at night and feeding her addictions to alcohol and cocaine. With tired legs and no place to go, Cindy sank hopelessly into a deep depression. One day she sat on a swing, feeling abandoned and alone. "Why is God not helping me?" she wondered. Were there no answers?

A week later, Cindy noticed an advertisement for a health center called The Rainbow Healing Room. When she dialed its telephone number, she learned about a lecture being given on the subject of a precious Mayan artifact. Spontaneously, she purchased a ticket and went. The meeting hall was packed with people milling about. The rest of the crowd faded into a blur as she noticed a particular man who came into focus no matter where she turned. "What's the matter?" he asked kindly when they finally met. "You don't look well. Would you take a walk with me after the program?"

"I don't think so," replied Cindy. "I want to be alone."

"You can be alone with me," he answered cryptically.

Cindy relented, and, as she reports, "We walked and we talked. I hugged a tree and I cried."

Eventually, Rick managed to convince Cindy to try algae, which she ate sporadically. Their relationship grew, and they moved into an apartment together. Discovering that she was pregnant catapulted her into consciousness about her health and that of her unborn child. Rick insisted that his baby have the benefit of algae during Cindy's pregnancy, and so she slowly worked up to eating approximately forty capsules a day. When Cindy was six months along, she and Rick decided to marry.

Cindy's gynecologist predicted that she might not be able to birth her baby with an intact cervix because of a previous problem in this area. So she exercised regularly by walking three miles a day and ate a well balanced diet including a daily handful of algae. During this time, her serum iron count rose and her attitude about life changed dramatically.

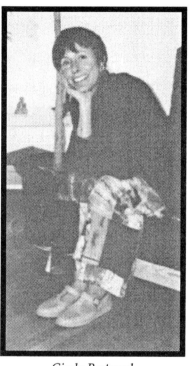

*Cindy Bertrand
looking and feeling terrific!*

Despite the doctor's grim prediction, Cindy's well-planned home birth exceeded their expectations. Her strong, healthy body performed smoothly, and their perfect baby boy, Jonathan, slid into the world without complication.

Unfortunately, Cindy Bertrand-Brodzik and her husband Rick separated and divorced four years later. Though their marriage was not destined to continue, they consciously chose to maintain a harmonious relationship for the benefit of their son. Cindy feels that Jonathan suffered less than he might have during this time because of his parants' commitment to a peaceful divorce.

A few months before they separated, Cindy bought her husband's Cell Tech business and has continued to expand it by telling others about the algae because she wishes to share the hope and joy it has given her. Her younger sister, who also had been addicted to drugs, recently telephoned her to tell her that she is now clean and sober and wants to follow Cindy in sharing Super Blue Green Algae with others. Cindy says her "heart sings" as she lies down to sleep at night when she thinks of the relatives she has helped. She feels a profound sense of gratitude for the blessings in her own life and the lives of her family members.

During the five years that it has taken for Cindy to feel spiritually strong, emotionally solid, and vitally healthy, she experienced several cleansing episodes. Because of the toxic chemicals she had poured into her body over the years, she needed to discharge and release their residue. The long and winding road to health has brought her an integration of body, mind, and spirit through sensible life-style changes. Today, her sparkling eyes and her happy smile testify to her return to wellness.

A pivotal moment for Cindy Bertrand was a life-changing, transformational event that marked a shift in consciousness for her as it has for many: Cindy met Daryl Kollman, cofounder of Cell Tech. His obvious joy was contagious, something she felt compelled to share.

A final comment from Cindy points out the disconnectedness in the world, especially in large cities. She watches people hurrying about the streets of Toronto and riding the subway to their jobs in their high-rise office buildings. Their busy feet seldom, if ever, touch the bare ground. Sharing algae with the people of Toronto fills Cindy with hope as she thinks of them "putting a piece of the earth into their bodies." In this way, we might all feel a little more connected, and eventually experience more peace in our lives.

Cindy Bertrand
Toronto, Canada

Marion Jones

Life was a merry-go-round for Marion. She dragged herself off to work every morning, came home exhausted at the end of each day, and tumbled into bed by eight o'clock every evening. Invariably, after a restless night and trouble sleeping, Marion would extract herself from bed around eight in the morning and begin the whole cycle again. She had no appetite and experienced constant discomfort. Irritable bowel complaints and other colon problems kept her seeing a gastroenterologist for several years. A rheumatologist labelled her assortment of symptoms with various -*itis* names, and prescribed the associated medications.

In mid-March last year, Marion's daughter gave her a very special gift for her birthday: a Sure Start Program from Cell Tech. (This kit contains acidophilus, plant enzymes, and two algae products.) Marion was unreceptive for two reasons: first, the magnitude of her health problems seemed out of the reach of a simple food, and second, she was wary of that "network marketing" word. Because her thirty-four year old daughter had noticed changes in her own allergy symptoms and had fewer headaches, increased skin tone, and an improved mental attitude, Marion tried to be open-minded. "It won't work for a body as broken as mine, but I'll give it a try," she thought.

Amazingly, Marion saw a difference within five days. Her bowel irritation, after plaguing her for six years, left completely. By three weeks into the program, this ball of energy was rising every morning by 6:30 and tackling housecleaning chores with a vengeance. Some of these tasks were activities she had been unable to perform without help for years. Even more importantly, Marion noticed her attitude improving, "The sun was shining in my life again — something that had been missing for years!" She began to exercise, became more fit, and watched her body composition change. She also accomplished something she had never done before, "After raking leaves in my yard, I went to a friend's house that very day and raked up five bags for her!"

Because of these changes, when Marion finished the contents of the Sure Start Program, she decided she was well enough to discontinue the algae altogether. Within four days, her bowel symptoms returned. She vowed never to let the bottles become empty again.

After a couple of months with the algae, Marion also noticed that a skin problem from which she suffered was disappearing too. She rarely had to deal with the awful itching. The feeling of having a rock stuck in her stomach area began to leave, and she was able to eat meals comfortably again. Several months into the program, the pain in her hips and knees diminished, and she seldom suffers from her previous joint stiffness.

One more development brought Marion an unexpected respite. For two years, she had suffered from a persistent infection in her throat. This led to constant laryngitis which caused her to miss valuable work time. Marion reports that for the past year and a half, she has not experienced this problem at all. "Unless you've suffered from something as frustrating as this, you can't even imagine what a relief it is."

Marion recognizes that food doesn't cure any medical condition, but that supplying her body with previously missing nutrients has produced profound changes in her mental, emotional, and physical health. "I have a life!" she cries ecstatically. "I *feel* as if I'm ten years younger than fifty-six."

"My [entire] family now eats the products," she says. "Even though several of them haven't experienced any earth-shattering effects, they *know* that they are putting something really powerful into their bodies every single day. I'm a walking testament to that!"

Marion Jones
El Dorado, Arkansas

Nila Bornstein

According to Greek mythology, there once lived a precocious young girl name Arachne, who spun and wove so skillfully that she challenged the goddess Athena to a contest. When Arachne produced a magnificent cloth, Athena flew into such a rage that she tore the material into pieces. In despair, the young maiden attempted to hang herself, but the goddess took pity on her and turned her into a spider.

Skillful spinners and weavers, spiders are classified as *Arachnida*, or arachnids, after the hapless girl in the tale above. The only two poisonous varieties in North America are the black widow and the violin spiders, the most well known of which is the brown recluse. While these hermits only bite when provoked, they can be fatal to a small child and will cause a crater-like wound that takes months to heal in a fully grown adult.

At 5'2" and 105 pounds, Nila Bornstein weighed in somewhere between a large child and a small adult. When she received a bite from a brown recluse spider, she became extremely ill. Nila chose to convalesce using herbal blood purifiers and water fasts instead of medication. Slowly, she began to recover, but her former vitality remained elusive. She spent weeks in bed, with no energy and little motivation.

Hearing about Nila's situation, a friend suggested that she try Super Blue Green Algae. Though Nila was still bedridden, she refused to consider it. She had been consuming Spirulina for ten years, liked it, and couldn't imagine that Cell Tech Super Blue Green Algae would offer her anything more. "No," she insisted. "I like Spirulina; that's not for me."

After watching her friend languish in bed for three weeks, Nila's concerned colleague telephoned her with the following message, "You're my friend, Nila, and you are going to find some algae in your mailbox today." Sure enough, when Nila's husband went to the mail room, an algae care package awaited him. He found acidophilus, enzymes, Omega Sun and

Alpha Sun.

Believing herself to be reasonably healthy, despite her present predicament, Nila began with five Alpha Sun and five Omega Sun capsules daily, in addition to the probiotics and enzymes. Three days later, she says she "popped out of bed, exclaiming, 'Oh, I remember *me*! This is how *I* feel — energetic and happy!' "

Nila improved quickly after adding Super Blue Green Algae to her diet. She feels that the algae has allowed her to assume tasks that a year ago would have been unthinkable. This hardy species of blue-green algae has survived through the ages and imparts its endurance factor to all who consume it. Nila Bornstein will be forever grateful to her special friend for introducing her to the miracle of Super Blue Green Algae.

Because of her desire to continue eating and sharing this marvelous food, Nila has become a Cell Tech distributor. Since her newfound exuberance came to her as a gift from a caring friend, Nila encourages everyone to share the algae with people who need it.

Nila Bornstein
Nevada City, California

Wayne Myers

It seemed to Wayne Myers that he was always on the road. As a traveling salesman, he spent a great deal of time in fast-food and hotel restaurants. Wayne's diet was unhealthy by any standards. His wandering life-style also produced other stresses.

When Wayne's company was purchased by another enterprise that already had enough salesmen, he was out of a job. For the next six months he searched for other employment, yet he suddenly spent

Wayne Myers with his caring and supportive new wife, Eva.

most of his time at home. His sudden, massive mood swings frightened him into seeing his medical doctor, who referred him to a local psychiatrist. The doctor offered a fancy diagnosis to describe the high and low mental roller-coaster that Wayne rode constantly. Finally, unable to cope with his unpredictable emotional extremes, his wife of sixteen years packed her bags and left.

Wayne dwelled longer in the troughs of his roller-coaster ride: plenty of lows, not many highs. He even contemplated suicide. To provide some relief, his physician increased his medication. When it became ineffective, it had to be alternated with another prescription. Now Wayne had a tennis match of back and forth pharmaceuticals to balance his up and down emotional thrill ride.

Exhausted, Wayne wanted off. He found a new physician who treated him for food allergies and worked with his diet.

The doctor recommended less protein and more vegetables. Then, sensing other problems, the doctor referred Wayne to a urologist, who discovered that Wayne had a significant loss of kidney function.

Wayne came in contact with Super Blue Green Algae shortly thereafter. He began eating four Alpha Sun and four Omega Sun each day. After thirty days, he began enjoying a normal night's rest instead of sleeping eighteen to twenty hours each day. He emerged from the dense mental fog he had been shrouded in to find his lost energy returning. This previously unemployed, emotional basket case returned to work for four hours a day.

Wayne's physician seemed pleased and hopeful, and he encouraged Wayne to continue eating his algae. Since that time, Wayne has worked diligently to develop a healthier diet and has had no more trouble with mood swings. He feels that a regular exercise program and a conscious effort at maintaining a positive mental attitude have also contributed to his improvement. Wayne is convinced that a return to emotional well-being requires a multifaceted approach, of which nutrition is one prong. A balanced, complete food such as Super Blue Green Algae rounds out his dietary requirements.

Two years after including algae in his health program, Wayne Myers has been given a reprieve: With improved kidney function, his urologist released him from care, and at his most recent yearly checkup, his medical doctor declared him more fit than most men his age. Wayne has happily remarried and says his desire to remain healthy has been his main catalyst for change.

Wayne Myers
Kirkland, Washington

Mary Votel

Born in 1950, Mary Votel grew up as a typical child of the baby boom generation. Her parents subscribed to traditional medical models of health care, so Mary was weaned early and raised on canned foods. As hippy teenagers of the 1960s, she and her peers sampled a smorgasbord of recreational drugs, imagining they would be invincible forever.

Following an extensive dental procedure in 1984, Mary Votel's world came crashing down around her shoulders. A severe bone infection left her with recurrent fevers, lymphatic swelling, and excruciating joint symptoms. This active and involved mother of four children between the ages of three months and ten years suddenly found herself incapacitated. Hardly able to walk or talk, she grimly wrote out her last will and testament.

Committee meetings and civic involvement ground to a halt. The only group she forced herself to attend was comprised of families with children who had difficulties focusing in school. Because her middle child suffered from this disability, Mary felt a strong need to stay connected.

One evening, a local chiropractor who had endured an attention disorder for most of his life gave a talk at Mary's monthly gathering. Dr. Haselden spoke about a wonderful, wild food that had provided him with increased mental clarity and an ability to concentrate for the first time. Mary waited patiently after the presentation to speak personally with Dr. Haselden. Super Blue Green Algae sounded as if it might help her, too, but she was doubtful. Having already exhausted thousands of dollars searching for a magic bullet, she had nothing left to spend on a product whose efficacy seemed questionable. Dr. Haselden, a warm and generous man, insisted on providing Mary with an initial supply of Super Blue Green Algae without charge. He knew she would benefit from eating this perfect food, and he wanted her to try it immediately.

Within twenty-four hours of eating the algae, Mary experienced an exciting change in her body. For the first time in seven years, she stood straight and tall without discomfort. Three days after her first algae capsule, Mary Votel took her four energetic children to Disney World, where she out-walked them for seven hours. Jared, the youngest, had never seen his mother without disability, and here she was surpassing them all!

Because Mary had been regularly using prescription and recreational drugs for twenty-nine years, she endured periodic detoxification as her body released these accumulated chemicals. At one point, she required sinus surgery to relieve the pressure from mucous buildup, and her lung area continues to clear. Mary has discovered that chlorophyll, the chemical that imparts its green color to the algae, is an effective cleansing agent. Eliminative organs work overtime to discharge poisons through all available channels. Some people may experience digestive cleansing, perspiration, headaches, and other symptoms as the body purges itself. This is normal and desirable.

As Mary began to emerge from her cocoon, her children took notice. They had watched helplessly as she rapidly deteriorated following the bone infection. When they added the algae to their diets, they also noticed a difference.

Amber, the oldest, is seventeen and very active in sports. She has decreased her running time as a result of her improved nutrition, and finds that her skin remains clear when she eats the acidophilus regularly. Her younger sister, who previously agonized over difficulty focusing in school, has achieved greater mental clarity and concentration. She no longer requires medication to control behavior problems and she continues to improve daily. Medical reports show that Mary's youngest daughter, who had been suffering from a progressive skeletal deficiency, is now experiencing bone remineralization.

Finally, Jared, the little boy born just three months before Mary began her spiralling descent into ill health, has also changed. Mary recalls how many times she related to others that her illness began shortly after Jared's birth. To Jared, this meant that he was somehow responsible for his mothers sickness. Ravaged by guilt and frustration, he began purposefully hurting himself. During this time, fourteen friends and members of the Votel family died, which Mary believes may have also contributed to Jared's feelings of helplessness and confusion. As his mother gained strength, Jared also became

> *"He no longer turns on himself out of despair and a desire for self-punishment."*

calmer and happier. He no longer turns on himself out of despair and a desire for self-punishment.

Peace rests over the household now, and life holds new hope for them all.

Mary Votel
St. Cloud, Florida

Amy Phillips

"I was the youngest of three girls born to a severely ill mother. After my birth, she was diagnosed with a degenerative neurological condition complicated by intense psychological problems. My mother was sick for as long as I can recall. During the time I knew her, I don't ever remember her walking. She died when I was twenty.

"Living in a dysfunctional family, I received constant physical, mental, spiritual, and emotional abuse. This, and the stress of essentially growing up without a mother, threw my body so out of balance that my health began to deteriorate.

"I suffered repeated ear infections and tonsil problems as a young child, each requiring repeated rounds of antibiotics. In my teens, I developed various skin disorders. At sixteen, I noticed a fungal rash on my abdomen which a dermatologist dismissed by telling me to bathe more regularly and wash my clothes more often. I discovered that climate and clothing materials affected the severity of my skin condition. For over twenty-five years, I showered twice a day just to keep the rash under control.

"As I grew older, my health declined even further. For instance, I often stopped breathing in my sleep for forty seconds at a time. Also, I frequently had diarrhea due to persistent bowel irritation; the fungus infection on my abdomen began to spread throughout my system; and, as a result of persistent joint stiffness and debilitating muscle inflammation, I spent a great deal of time bedridden. By this time, my body was so depleted that I had become chronically fatigued. I slept twelve to fourteen hours a day, awoke tired, and took a nap later in the afternoon. For years I itched so badly during the night that I woke up bloody from scratching.

"In addition to my physical problems, new memories of my childhood abuse began to surface. The stress became so severe that I could hardly cope. A minimal back injury totally disabled me and I had to quit my job. Though I tried every avenue, from traditional medicine to acupuncture, I could find no relief. No matter what I did, nothing helped.

"Severe abdominal pain resulted in two surgeries. Following the second operation, I sank into a deep depression. As I spiralled downward, I searched one last time for answers to my ever increasing health problems.

"Fortunately, I turned to a holistic doctor who rescued me from spinning out of control. He discovered a systemic yeast infection and a sensitivity to wheat gluten. My intestines were so severely weakened that toxins were leaking into my body. Hence the skin problems. By targeting the yeast overgrowth with antifungal agents and modifying my diet, my doctor helped me to bring my body back into balance.

"I also learned about Super Blue Green Algae. One day, as I flipped through our local paper while bedridden, I noticed an advertisement for a home-based business opportunity. I had wondered what I could do to be productive from my sick bed. When I telephoned the number in the newspaper, I realized that not only had I found a business opportunity, but I'd found a potential answer to my health challenges as well.

"After beginning the Sure Start program of acidophilus, enzymes, and Omega and Alpha Sun, I noticed immediate results. I was awestruck at my body's reaction. The first day, I experienced bursts of energy. I felt uplifted, lighter. By the end of the week, I was strong enough to drive all the way to Los Angeles, California from Flagstaff, Arizona to attend a Super Blue Green weekend hosted by Cell Tech. Daryl and Marta Kollman were there, and I heard repeated testimonials from others whose lives had been changed by eating this incredible food.

"It amazes me how some basic changes in my nutritional habits have transformed my life, too. My depression has lifted, and my rash is gone. No more fungus problems! Best of all, I only require six to eight hours of sleep instead of twelve to fourteen. That's like having an extra day in my day!

"At forty-three years old, I have returned to hiking, with energy left over to care for our two special needs foster children. I work an average of thirty-five hours a week with developmentally disabled youngsters, and I have a terrific husband and five lovely feline companions.

"My memory is sharper and my mind is clearer. Things that have baffled me for years suddenly make sense. Most importantly, the spiritual work I have been struggling with just comes naturally to me now. I wake up and perceive God. I feel connected for the first time in my life. When I walk outside without shoes, I actually sense the energy of the earth underneath my feet.

"I was headed down the same road my mother had taken so disastrously before me, when everything suddenly changed. Enter the algae! Enter my new life!

"With the experiences of my husband (who had severe attention and focus problems), the improvements in the special needs children we work with, the incredible changes in myself and in our five cats, I cannot imagine *not* sharing what we have learned with others. We feel it is our duty now. . .and that we have been led here just for this."

Amy Phillips
Flagstaff, Arizona

Note: Amy's holistic doctor is now an algae-eater too. Impressed with the wonderful changes he observed in Amy, he signed up with her to become a Cell Tech distributor.

Norman Womack

Dr. Dean Ornish's book, *Reversing Heart Disease*, provided Norman Womack with a blueprint for his new life. The Cardiac Rehabilitation Unit at the Veterans Hospital in Buffalo, New York, also recommended a specific exercise program. This he followed at the Corning YMCA with his personal trainer.

Norman Womack

At the start of each session, the trainer strapped a blood pressure monitor and pulse meter to Norman's left biceps as he warmed up on an exercise bike. Often, he experienced a telltale pain down his arm that dissipated as he continued his warm-up. If the discomfort continued, he would cool down and end his session.

In the autumn of 1994, one year after Norman began his rehabilitation program, his special friend, Sera Smolen, called to inform him of a fabulous nutritional product. Sera was a vegetarian and extremely health conscious. For some time she had been using Spirulina, a type of blue-green algae grown in artificial conditions, but now that she had encountered Super Blue Green Algae, she noticed a far greater improvement in her health and vitality.

Norman had been living on welfare checks and protested that his meager funds would scarcely cover the cost of the proposed nutritional program. "It has a 60-day, money back guarantee, Norman," she cajoled. When she offered to buy him his algae with her credit card and take payments in return,

Norman could hardly refuse her generosity.

The shipment arrived just after Christmas and Norman began eating his algae right away. Immediately, he experienced strong cleansing: He vomited for two days, and then had diarrhea for two more. When he reported this to Sera, she questioned him as to the amount he had eaten. He replied that he had taken just two each of Alpha Sun and Omega Sun. She believed that his body was so depleted that it couldn't metabolize the concentrated superfood without help. Because Norman was on a fixed income, Sera had, against her better judgment, agreed to start him on the algae without the digestive aids. "Stop eating the algae, immediately," she said. "I'll order the acidophilus and enzymes for you as a Christmas gift." She had suggested the Sure Start Program* (acidophilus, enzymes, Omega Sun and Alpha Sun) from the very beginning, but Norman had balked at the cost. And so, Norman began again.

Heart-related difficulties were not the only health challenges from which he suffered. Years of physical decline were evidenced by the stiffness in his hands; inflammation of his left shoulder; digestive complaints such as a raw, irritated stomach; flatulence and constant vacillation between constipation and diarrhea; energy slumps; mood swings; and an unsightly rash on his face and scalp. These were all signs of many years of nutritional imbalance and an unconscious lifestyle.

Once Norman launched his new and improved algae program, he noticed changes instantly. The first area to improve was his digestive tract. As this is often the site where degenerative disease begins (through absorption and elimination difficulties), it was natural that this system would be the first to revive. One morning, Norman noticed that the rash and exfoliating skin on his face and scalp seemed less severe. He discontinued his daily application of a special cream to see if the symptoms would return. They did not. "As my energy level began to climb, my afternoon slumps went away, and

*Available from Cell Tech.

with them disappeared the highs and lows of the mood swings. I also felt an increase in stamina during my workouts."

At the beginning of the second week, Norman added Alpha Sun algae to his probiotics and enzymes, and the third week he included the Omega Sun. He was now utilizing the full program with no ill effects. Elated by the changes he had experienced so far, Norman hardly expected the following additional surprise: During his first workout in the fourth week of the Sure Start Program, his trainer placed

> *"What feelings?" he shouted joyfully. "They're gone!"*

the monitor on his arm as usual before he began his warm up. Norman pumped his legs on the exercycle, breathed deeply, and noticed no pressure on his chest or down his arm. He felt great! More importantly, his startled trainer perceived something even better. While his pulse increased, his blood pressure remained constant. Norman peddled harder. Still he had no discomfort and no change in his blood pressure. His pulse rose and sweat poured off of him. "Norm," she cautioned, "take it easy until we get past the feelings in your chest and arm."

"What feelings?" he shouted joyfully. "They're gone!"

Shortly thereafter, Norman ran out of his algae. Too broke and too embarrassed to ask his sponsor for help, he procrastinated and went without. Gradually, his symptoms reappeared, causing concern to himself and his personal trainer. Finally, he called Sera and confessed his predicament to her. She provided him with more algae, and a week later, his trainer watched the monitor carefully and then dropped her jaw in amazement when she saw that everything had returned to normal.

Norman's medical doctor listened carefully as he described the wonderful changes he had experienced. Once the doctor had ascertained that his energetic protege had altered nothing else about his diet or life-style, he expressed his opinion that Super Blue Green Algae had offered the nutritional missing link Norman had been looking for.

Norman passed on some literature and a tape called "The Physiology of the Algae"* to his flabbergasted physician. Several other doctors in his town have requested information and are open to the possible advantages of improved nutrition for their clientele. Norman continues to improve and to spread the word in Corning, New York.

Norman Womack
Corning, New York

---

* Available through Cell Tech.

Consuelo Luz Arostegui

For ten years, Consuelo had experienced incapacitating fatigue, flu-like symptoms, and rashes. It all began with a hospital stay for an emergency appendectomy, which resulted in a downward spiral in her immune function. Afterwards, her mental focus and concentration fragmented, leaving her frequently depressed and overwhelmed.

There were a few bright spots during those years. Consuelo and her husband, Jeff, raised a family and also created their own business, a radio network company. Although fatigued most of the time, Consuelo forced herself to write, perform, record music albums, and host a daily radio show that aired nationally.

Consuelo's despair came from the unpredictability of her "fatigue attacks," as she refers to them. "Out of the blue, I would suddenly feel as if someone had pulled the plug on my source of life and energy." Drained and depleted, Consuelo sometimes found herself prostrate on the floor, as if trying desperately to soak up some life from Mother Earth herself. These spells continued for one to three hours and occurred several times a month. The resultant headachy flu could last for days. For fear of being stricken on stage, she refused to make any definite performance plans.

One day, Consuelo received a golden opportunity to perform her one-woman musical play on the life of the poet, Gabriela Mistral, in the finest theater in Santa Fe, New Mexico. Although she was nervous about her health, she accepted the invitation. Her mother flew all the way from Spain for this special event. On the night of the gala performance, three hours before curtain time, disaster struck. Consuelo suddenly collapsed and lay semiconscious on the floor of her studio for what seemed like an eternity. Finally, one hour before curtain time, Consuelo roused herself. With superhuman effort, she dragged herself through the play, barely projecting her voice and struggling to control her emotions. The audience in the back of the theater shouted for her to speak up, but try as she might, her vocal chords would not cooperate. The show director was furious. He knew how powerfully she had performed at rehearsal the day before, and he failed to understand the change. As so often happened, other people believed Consuelo's condition to be psychological rather than physiological. She was embarrassed, humiliated, and exhausted.

Consuelo stopped performing. She continued her endless round of doctors, alternative treatments, and supplements to no avail. Medication controlled some of her complaints, but the debilitating fatigue continued. As she remembers, "I was easily overwhelmed, and I found it difficult to get organized. Planning and [arranging] my son Max's Bar Mitzvah was a real challenge!"

Several years later, a therapist friend of Consuelo's suggested Super Blue Green Algae. Always open minded, Consuelo ordered the products immediately and began with the digestive aids — probiotic intestinal bacteria and enzymes.

With the introduction of the Cell Tech products, Consuelo's life changed dramatically. For the first time in her long ordeal, she "woke up rested, filled with energy, and overjoyed about life." She experienced mental clarity and focus for the first time in ten years. "I am exercising again. I swim or jog for forty minutes five to seven days a week." When she does feel fatigued or experience a headache, the severity is far less. With a little rest, her strength returns. "It's as if my immune system has finally kicked in and is able to do its job!"

In the past, Consuelo had tried Spirulina, a cultivated blue-green algae product, but felt no change in her health. She says, "There was something in the Super Blue Green Algae that felt different — something that my body was obviously lacking — something almost miraculous. The only way you can experience the power of this algae is to try it. I felt my consciousness actually change as the algae seemed to help me become more aware of my body and what it truly needs.

"With our radio network business booming and making a more generous income than I ever imagined, I certainly wasn't looking for another business. But I am so excited about the algae and what it has done for me that I truly want to share it with the world. I also intend to create a fund with the business profits that will enable me to help others.

"I hope that my story will encourage [people] to try Super Blue Green Algae. Of course, you don't have to be sick to benefit from [it]. Everyone can use increased health, energy, and mental and physical well-being!"

Consuelo Luz Arostegui is now performing again and plans to record a new compact disc very soon.

Consuelo Luz Arostegui
Santa Fe, New Mexico

Bonnie Thain

Breast-feeding a seven month old and chasing an active two and a half year old often requires superhuman energy. As a twenty-four year old, stay-at-home mom with two children under three, Bonnie Thain relies on the stamina she receives from eating Super Blue Green Algae.

After eating algae for a little while, Bonnie noticed that she could get up during the night with her children and still awaken rested in the morning. The "slump" in the afternoon, which usually culminated in a nap, quickly disappeared.

Bonnie grew up in a health conscious household. Her mother is a massage and colon therapist who has always embraced the natural healing model. Bonnie's mother introduced her to Super Blue Green Algae while they were sharing a visit together in her home in Florida. "She would put some by my plate at meals, and I ate it because I knew if my mother was eating it, then it must be something good!" says Bonnie, trustingly.

That summer, Bonnie and her mother spent several days at the beach with the grandchildren in tow. The young mother had been experiencing a decrease in her milk flow that didn't respond to any alterations Bonnie made in her diet or lifestyle. After eating algae regularly for several days in a row (Mother was very persistent and consistent), Bonnie felt a change. As she walked along the beach, suddenly her breasts filled with milk. This surprising event repeated itself several times during the day. She couldn't believe it! As long as Bonnie continued to eat her algae, she maintained a steady supply of nourishment for her growing baby.

One day she ran out of algae, and again her milk supply began to dwindle. Daily consumption of algae results in an abundance of milk for a very happy Caitlin.

Bonnie also observed a shift in body proportion after about five months of eating her algae. She was finally pleased with the image in the mirror.

After seven months of eating algae, Bonnie discovered that her allergic reactions to dogs had diminished. All her life she had broken out in hives on any part of her skin that touched a dog. If she petted a dog and then rubbed her eyes, they would swell and itch. One day a dog came to visit their family and Bonnie stroked him with-

> *"I can express myself and stand up for myself much better."*

out thinking. Amazingly, her previously sensitive skin remained clear. As an experiment, she rolled up her sleeves and spread her bare arms all over the potential allergen. She even rubbed her fingers into her eyes. No reaction! "It's wonderful to be able to pet a dog, now. I've missed that all my life!" she confesses.

An unusual side-benefit from adding a source of high quality nutrients to Bonnie's diet is her newfound self-confidence. "I can express myself and stand up for myself much better. I struggled with this problem for years, and the algae has really helped me to overcome my fear." She also deals with stress more productively.

Occasionally, Bonnie experiences various symptoms of cleansing or detoxification. This pleases her because she believes that the flushing action helps clean out a lifetime of built-up chemicals and debris.

What a gift for Bonnie to experience greater health and well-being from this wild superfood. "Sharing this beautiful food with others is so rewarding. I especially enjoy watching [people] add *life* [through eating wild-grown algae] to their lives, and I am privileged to offer them the same financial freedom I now have. I am so thankful for Super Blue Green Algae!"

Bonnie Thain
Dalton, Georgia

Lauri Burgdorff

Health improvements can be subtle when brought about by dietary change. Lauri Burgdorff's story illustrates this.

"I am the kind of person who comes down with colds easily," she admits. A few late nights or stress from any source invariably lowers her resistance to the point of instant illness. Lauri attributes this to aller-

Lauri Burgdorff and friend.

gies and an unusually high need for sleep.

Last year was especially challenging for Lauri. After working excessively long hours, she became ill with a respiratory infection that took six weeks of recovery. She was ready to try anything when a friend at work presented her with a tape about Super Blue Green Algae.

She began eating algae shortly after returning from a long business trip and her sister's wedding. As if waiting for the proverbial shoe to drop, she expected the inevitable illness to arrive anytime. A week went by, then two. After three weeks of diligently eating the algae without sniffling, Lauri noticed short bursts of unanticipated energy. By the fourth week, she gave it the ultimate test: For four nights in a row, our previous early-nighter stayed up until midnight, without any repercussions. Instead of sleeping until her alarm sounded, Lauri began to awaken at 5:30 in the morning feeling refreshed and ready for her day.

Life itself somehow seemed easier. In one week, Lauri

needed to replace two broken major appliances. While this would have been a recipe for stress in the past, this time she handled it like a pro. Shortly thereafter, Lauri underwent a "rough career transition." She amazed her colleagues with her newly acquired ability to slide calmly on through. Better nutrition was definitely affecting her attitude.

Living in Connecticut with its frigid winters, Lauri was unable to survive an entire winter without illness of some kind. At the time she recounted her story, Lauri had experienced half the winter months without a cold or flu. She can now also stay up until eleven or twelve o'clock at night without feeling tired.

Many people who have a positive experience with Super Blue Green Algae choose to share it with their animal friends. Lauri Burgdorff's eleven year old German shepherd lacked energy, had undergone three surgeries, and was becoming senile. It was time for a canine algae program! After two weeks, the dog seemed less forgetful and appeared to have more energy. As of this writing, Lauri reports that her beloved shepherd is more frisky and affectionate, playing like a puppy every evening instead of flopping on the floor with fatigue.

"I am thrilled with this product and have been using it for five months. I cannot wait to see how it impacts my health year round." Neither can we, Lauri!

Lauri Burgdorff
Huntington, Connecticut

Dianne Marshall

Talented, vivacious, and energetic in high school, Dianne Marshall excelled at her favorite activities: singing and cheerleading. One summer, she spent her vacation on Catalina Island performing with Jerry Gray and his Band of Today, formerly Glen Miller's Orchestra. Another time, she was the featured singer for several weeks on a television show hosted by Jack Jones called Spotlight on Youth. She even auditioned to become a Mouseketeer on the Mickey Mouse Club. According to Dianne, she "lived to sing."

Abruptly, her dream evaporated. When Dianne began falling frequently, especially to the left, she knew that something was wrong, terribly wrong. Neurological tests and a spinal tap revealed various irregularities, but Dianne went on with her life and eventually her symptoms subsided.

Ten years later, while pregnant and struggling with a stressful marriage, Dianne again experienced similar nervous system disturbances. One day, following a heated argument, she turned quickly to leave when a black veil descended over her eyes. Disoriented and afraid, she screamed, "I can't see!" In the hospital at UCLA Medical Center, her neurologist asked her if she knew what might be causing her symptoms. Dianne had been reading about some chronic, degenerative conditions and ran off a list of ten signs that described a particular diagnosis. Some time after Thanksgiving, the same doctor confirmed her suspicion. "In a way, I was relieved," says Dianne. "The other choice would have been terminal. At least I could live with this."

Dianne wrestled with a crumbling marriage and constant health concerns. At one point, her two children were cruelly abducted for fifty-nine long days. They were told that their mother was dead and would never come back. Dianne was consumed with worry, which only added to the stress affecting her health. She searched everywhere for her precious children, and when she finally found them, she made a firm resolution that no one would ever take them away again. No matter what the condition of her health, she would always protect and care for them.

Her fight and her determination carried her through the rigors of a physically challenged life. Over the years, she endured a sequence of surgeries to alleviate facial neuralgia and suffered repeatedly with overwhelming fatigue. Fortunately, her positive mental attitude sustained her in difficult times.

Two years ago, Dianne's brother and best friend called her from California on a particularly depressing day. "Is there anything I can do for you?" he asked. "Anything at all?"

"I'm feeling so sick and tired," she replied. "Just get me something to make me feel better."

Two days later, he called her back to say that a friend of his would be contacting her with information about something called Super Blue Green Algae.

Four days after eating her first algae tablets, Dianne walked to the bathroom for the first time, unaided. She remarked to her brother, who was visiting her at the time, that she felt better, stronger, and more hopeful. He just nodded his head and smiled!

When Dianne strode into her neurologist's office without help, he exclaimed, "Look at you! What are you doing?" Her skin radiated a rosy glow, and she was walking better. Without hesitation she responded by telling him about the wonderful, nutrient-dense food that she had added to her diet. Since then, she has committed to sharing the algae with other people experiencing similar neurological conditions.

Only three months later, Dianne danced with her son at a friend's daughter's wedding. The circle of onlookers understood the significance of this occurrence and broke into applause when the music stopped. They were all amazed and wanted to hear about the many exciting changes she had experienced in her health.

The same year, Dianne planned and executed her mother's 80th birthday party. Because she had previously been a professional singer, she promised her mother that she would sing a special song for her. For the first time in fourteen years,

Dianne arranged and sang the song, "Young at Heart." How appropriate!

Still, Dianne had a final obstacle to perfect health. Because of extensive degeneration in her spine, Dianne required a delicate three hour operation. Although the doctors questioned her ability to handle such a procedure with her prior neurological history, Dianne surprised everyone by "sailing through." Her only demand upon entering the hospital was that she be allowed to bring her algae.

Subsequent surgery on Dianne's shoulder to remove bone spurs and a portion of her collar bone required another hospital stay. Once again, Dianne amazed everyone with her short recovery. Eight days after her operation, this determined fighter demonstrated to her physician how much movement she had reacquired in her shoulder.

"Look Doc!" she exclaimed. "Look what I can do!"

"No one comes into my office eight days post-op doing what you're doing," he replied, shaking his head in disbelief.

"*I* can," emphasized Dianne, "because I eat algae!"

Throughout her many ordeals, Dianne has maintained a positive, upbeat attitude. Presently, she moves better, has more energy, and looks forward to her future with enthusiasm and hope. Although at times she has been blind, deaf, and unable to walk, today, her health continues to improve.

As Dianne says enthusiastically, "They can never take my dignity, and they can never take my fight." And don't try to take away her algae, either!

Dianne Marshall
Highlands Ranch, Colorado

Katharine Clark

Katharine Clark just turned forty years old on Saint Patrick's day this year. Yet inside this warm and compassionate woman beats the heart of a sixteen year old girl, tempered by the wisdom of someone way beyond her years. Katharine has lived a challenging but rewarding life, and while she has given much, she has so much more to give. Here is her story.

The year is 1983. Katharine and her partner have established a nonprofit organization that teaches about alternative energy for the home and educates others about all aspects of growing food indoors. Their business is expanding rapidly and they often fly around the world to spread the word.

Katharine's friend, Showshawme, calls her from Hawaii several times to tell her about a powerful superfood. "You should really try this Super Blue Green Algae from Cell Tech," he insists.

Katharine relates, "To get him off my back, I finally relented."

While on a promotional tour outside the Untied States some time later, Katharine runs out of the algae and realizes how different she feels. Upon returning home, Katharine immediately calls Showshawme to request more algae. Unfortunately, his telephone number has been changed and she doesn't locate him again for *five* years. During this time, Katharine's environmental business prospers, rising to a pinnacle of success. Her partner, in turn, sinks into the depths of despair, and finally suffers a mental breakdown. Without his support, their business folds. The very day after the doors closed for the last time, her mother and brother arrive at the facility to see her operation — her hugely successful venture. Mortified, Katharine can't bring herself to tell them of her loss. From there, she, too, spirals downward until she spends most of her time in bed, feeling depressed and hopeless.

One day, at the urging of their mutual friend Viktoras

Kulvinskas, Showshawme flies to Miami to pull Katharine from the pit into which she has fallen. Armed with his little bottle of liquid brain food (Omega Sun), he rushes to her rescue. Five minutes after he squirts some liquid Omega into Katharine's mouth, he looks at his watch and asks her if she notices any difference yet. Amazingly, she does! Her peripheral vision has cleared up, and she feels flushed with a sense of well-being. She suddenly feels more hopeful.

Katharine Clark

After explaining the entire distributor manual to Katharine, Showshawme quizzes her on its contents, and then takes her out on the town to tell everyone they meet about Super Blue Green Algae. Within two weeks, Katharine's attitude has turned around 180 degrees. She can see a future for herself, and it looks as if it might be happy and healthy.

Katharine feels so much stronger that she decides it is time to return to work. She updates her resume and sets out to tackle a number of job interviews. Upon completing the entire list, Katharine realizes that she has managed to sign up most of the interviewers as Cell Tech distributors. She just can't resist telling people how much better she feels, and why! With a growing network of people in her organization, she decides to make Cell Tech her career. The year is 1987.

In 1988, Katharine marries a handsome young man named Keen Jay who is the brother of a woman in Katharine's Cell Tech business. It is love at first sight for both of them!

Then in 1990, after extended travels around the world, the couple move their household possessions to a new home and have barely unpacked their things when disaster strikes: The day after the move, they are driving their van when it is hit by another vehicle. The van flips over and careens down the asphalt on its roof. Katharine sees Keen's forehead up against the windshield as the roadway scrapes by on the other side of the glass. He is unconscious, and she, too, blanks out shortly afterwards.

The paramedics arrive and with concerted effort extricate them from the mangled van. Insisting that they will be all right, Katharine and Keen Jay decline a trip to the emergency room. Instead, they consult with a holistic practitioner who treats them for their injuries and recommends strict bed rest. Concerned for her husband's safety, Katharine stays awake at night to make sure Keen is breathing well. She is worried about his injuries and ignores her own symptoms. Finally, she admits that she, too, needs attention. Ligaments and muscles were torn and bruised by the whipping motion of her neck, a concussion had caused her to lose consciousness, her ribs had been dislocated, and multiple bruises have popped up all over her body.

Katharine struggles to regain her energy and to reverse the effects of her injuries. Her main goal is to find the strength to participate in an exercise program to keep herself fit, something her doctor feels she will never be able to do again. Her condition deteriorates further. Without her former stamina, Katharine runs out of steam easily.

A year and a half later, Katharine and Keen travel to Hawaii for a Cell Tech event. While the rest of their group hikes up the volcanoes and enjoys the sights on the island, Katharine stays behind. Keen must drop her off at the entrance to a department store because she hasn't the energy to walk across the parking lot. Just to maintain herself at her present level, Katharine consumes one hundred Alpha and one hundred Omega capsules every day. Still, she often opens the refrigerator, sighs, and informs her husband that if she ate everything in it, she would still be hungry. One day, her friend Sue suggests that perhaps Katharine has parasites that are sapping her energy.

Upon returning to the mainland, Katharine consults a specialist who confirms that she is, indeed, infested with millions of round worms that are eating her meals faster than *she* can. In the doctor's opinion, it is only the massive quantities of algae that Katharine is ingesting that is keeping her alive. She recalls that she has had difficulties with low energy since childhood, and she suspects that parasites have been the cause. Her father owned a butcher shop when she was a young girl. She suspects that she may have contracted the worms through exposure to raw meat or by eating insufficiently cooked beef. The trauma of her auto accident had apparently lowered her immune function to such a level that the worm population grew unchecked. With the help of the appropriate medication, the parasitic infection is soon under control, and Katharine begins the long road to recovery.

Throughout all of Katharine's twists and turns, she has continued to eat her Super Blue Green Algae. Today she and her husband have a strong marriage and vibrantly healthy bodies. Katharine enjoys exercising again, even running up and down the stairs of their two-story home, just because she can. She maintains a dizzying schedule as a Cell Tech Relay 2000 trainer, which means that she and Keen spend more weekends in hotels than in their own home. Her Cell Tech organization continues to flourish, and she maintains a network of committed business people. Her monthly newsletter requires her personal attention, and she planned and organized the 1996 Cell Tech Winter Carnival cruise, as well as many other Cell Tech events. "I work because I want to, not because I have to," she says with enthusiasm.

Instead of requiring a nap every afternoon, Katharine finds that her energy level remains constant and she works right through her formerly normal slump. After her auto accident, Katharine's thyroid gland stopped functioning, but since she started eating algae, it has begun to produce hormones again. Now that she has resolved her health challenges, she eats her algae every day, exercises often, and maintains a joyous out-

look on life.
"I feel better at forty than I did at twenty!" she exclaims.

Katharine Clark
Atlanta, Georgia

Katherine's story brings to mind the last stanza of one of
my favorite poems:

I shall be telling this with a sigh
Somewhere ages and ages hence:
Two roads diverged in a wood, and I —
I took the one less traveled by,
And that has made all the difference.

Robert Frost

Captain Mike

The fifty year old, wizened tugboat captain squinted intently through his windshield at the driving snow. Never in his twenty-five years maneuvering the Atlantic Star around New York harbor had he worked in such a blizzard. The wind howled fiercely and the wall of flying snow obliterated his view.

Miguel Angel Figueroa, affectionately known as Captain Mike, had received his orders at 1800 hours the night before: move a light barge (420' long with a 70' beam and 30' of free board) through the Liberty Bridge and on to Stapleton anchorage. The big blizzard of 1996 had just departed, and the wary captain decided to check on the weather for the next morning. Winds of twenty-five to thirty knots were predicted; it didn't look promising, but if he didn't move the ship, its owner would lose valuable time and money. He took the contract.

By departure time, the gusty winds had approached a dangerous speed and heavy snow had begun. Captain Mike regretted accepting this assignment, but he had committed to it, so he continued on. The engine roared to life and the Atlantic Star inched out into the harbor.

By the time he reached the designated ship, the winds had picked up to a blinding seventy knots and the upper harbor rocked with choppy, six foot waves. Calmly and intently, Miguel secured his tugboat to the large seagoing vessel and began guiding it to safety. When he called his dispatcher to report on his whereabouts, the recalcitrant captain learned that his was the only remaining tugboat still in operation in the violent storm. Cool, collected and in control, Captain Mike focused on the job of expertly shepherding his charge to its destination, despite the angry tempest that raged about him. He marvelled at the confidence he felt.

The newfound personal power that this aging sea captain displayed while he stayed active in a job usually filled by much younger men could only have come from one source. Last November, Miguel Angel Figueroa began eating Super Blue Green Algae. He was familiar with health foods and vitamins because he had been previously supplementing his diet and watching what he ate. Though the high stress level of his occupation and erratic sleep patterns had taken their toll on his health, nutrient supplementation had provided some balance. Prior to the algae, Miguel had felt pressured by the demands of his work. Now he takes the daily grind and the lack of sleep in stride, feeling better than he has in years.

Four days of eating algae were all it took for Captain Mike to realize that he had come upon a superfood. Strength and vitality surged through him. His stress level is now manageable, and he sleeps soundly between his six-hour work shifts. He reports that he wakes up rested and refreshed with only four or five hours of sleep.

"I thought I was following my bliss to find Super Blue Green Algae," he says. "I have been blessed by it."

Miguel Angel Figueroa
"Captain Mike"
New York and Puerto Rico

Greg Neuburger

Greg Neuburger had been Steven Kasower's neighbor, friend, and gardener for ten years. For nearly two decades, Greg was an alcoholic, and like many imbibers, he failed to eat a balanced diet. In fact, during the last seven years, Steve had watched his friend's health gradually deteriorate as he subsisted on beer and Cheerios. Not much nutrition there!

When Greg found himself the victim of multiple bicycle accidents about which he remembered nothing, it frightened him into stopping alcohol completely. Withdrawal symptoms threw his body into a tailspin that confused and alarmed him. He grew so depressed that he attempted suicide. As a concerned neighbor and friend, Steven began to worry when Greg curled up in bed for days at a time without answering the door. When his insistent knocks were finally answered, Steve spent hours with Greg, visualizing health and wellness and supporting him through this difficult transition. However, Greg still woke up tired and listless in the morning, without motivation or enthusiasm for his day. Gradually, his gardening business fell apart. His doctors recommended medication to help his depression, but Greg was determined not to trade one chemical dependency for another.

One day, when Greg wouldn't open his door, Steve became adamant. Greg eventually let him in and Steve offered an ultimatum, "You eat this algae. It will give you a lift. I guarantee it! You will have more control over your life!" He knew that Greg was severely depleted nutritionally and felt that algae would help Greg to rebuild both his mind *and* his body. A still, small voice inside must have told Greg that Steve was making sense, because he finally accepted the algae.

Within two days, Mr. Fix-it arose at five o'clock in the morning and began repairing his deteriorating gardening equipment. He felt great! He had more energy, more verve, and he was raring to go! Then the bottom dropped out from under him. Years worth of toxins that had accumulated in the cells of his body all decided to evacuate the premises at once, or so it seemed to Greg. All orifices discharged simultaneously, alternating between diarrhea and vomiting, leaving their victim prostrate on the bathroom floor. Nothing stayed in his stomach except his algae.

Greg understood the cleansing process and tenaciously clung to his physical integrity and his sanity. Steve called his upline reinforcements and they all offered support for Greg's detoxification process. He came through with proverbial flying colors to emerge stronger, clearer, and more positive. Today, his outlook is upbeat and he doesn't feel depressed at the end of a tiring day. Greg exercises regularly, has resuscitated his business, and has even quit smoking. At one point, he sent a rather large invoice to his neighbor, Steve, for yard work done but not billed. While he had accomplished much of the physical labor during this time, Greg had fallen behind on his paperwork. The mental clarity that followed the addition of algae to his diet enabled him to bring the delinquent billing up to date. Steve checked his records and found that sure enough, he owed Greg a rather large sum of money. For him, Greg's new vitality carried a price. . . .

Oh well, as they say, "One man's loss is another man's gain," and in this case one might suggest, "One man's gain is another man's loss!"

Greg Neuburger continues to eat his Super Blue Green Algae products with life-enhancing results, and his neighbor, Steve, no longer has to worry about him. The only thing Steve worries about is his gardening bill!

Steven Kasower
Sacramento, California

Suki Baldwin

March was a double anniversary for Suzanne (Suki) Baldwin. It was her fortieth birthday, and she had been eating Super Blue Green Algae for exactly one year. "This was one of the happiest birthday celebrations of my life," she exclaimed, "not because forty is the *big one,* but because of the algae! Turning forty was a far cry from turning thirty-nine!"

Thirteen months before, Suki struggled with a sore hip for which she had consulted many health practitioners. In addition, she had used salves, ointments, exercises, vitamins, minerals, and homeopathic remedies, to no avail.

"In the meantime," recalls Suki, "my mother underwent hip replacement surgery. 'You know,' my mother said to me, 'I was about your age when my hip started bothering me.'

"That was a sort of *Welcome to the Club* I'd rather have done without, which I followed by a vow to myself that I would not put up with my pain for thirty-five years."

X-rays showed nothing significant, but an acupuncturist discovered a misalignment in her left ankle that he restored with an adjustment. She had immediate relief in her hip, but the correction didn't hold.

"Talk about discouraging!" laments Suki. "There I was, almost thirty-nine years old, barely able to climb stairs, capable only of taking short, easy walks with my children, not strong enough to lift or carry them, and imploring my husband to buy a flat house — no stairs or basement. Flat. *Please!*"

Suki had spent the last several years on a quest for health for herself and her family. Through nutrition and chiropractic care, she worked gradually to make changes in their physical health and mental attitudes. Her ill-health contributed to her constant irritability, and she desperately wanted to have more patience with her children. "I never added up how much money I was spending on supplements because I didn't want to tell my husband the amount. I kept searching because I still felt lousy."

One week before her thirty-ninth birthday, Suki listened to a cassette tape mailed to her several months earlier by a friend. "Wow!" she thought. "If this stuff is one fourth as good as they say it is, I need it, my dog needs it, and my family needs it!"

Suki Baldwin began eating Super Blue Green Algae, and, as she says, *kapowie!* Her life changed — and her hip

Suki Baldwin with husband Kevin and daughters Sally and Jeannie.

changed, too. Within six months, she could go up and down the stairs as often as she wanted, frequently running up two steps at a time. A year later, much of her discomfort was gone.

Within one hour of eating her first algae capsules, Suki began cleaning house. This was previously an unsavory task, and one she avoided whenever possible. That day, she got as much done as she usually did in a week! "Since I started eating the algae, I find myself more productive, more organized, faster in my work, and less easily distracted," she says enthusiastically. She has reached her goal of patience with her children, reacting more rationally with them and focusing on the positive. When in conflict with someone, Suki finds more options for resolution that benefit everyone.

"My chiropractor (also an algae eater!) notices how much better I am. I feel stronger, I get more things done, and I need less sleep. It is so wonderful to feel whole again. I can mow the lawn without having to wear a filter over my nose and mouth, I don't itch when I'm finished mowing, and my sensitivity to odors and foods has lessened. My concentration is more focused, and although I have always been a fast reader, I now read even faster. I feel like I have my *self* back, the girl I lost gradually between 1978 and 1995.

"Over the last five years, my marriage had seriously deteriorated. I spent most of the previous fall and winter trying to decide things such as, 'Do I move in with my mother or change the locks? Who gets the car? How will he pay child support? *Why can't we work things out anymore?!*' I loved my husband dearly, but had run out of patience in several areas of our relationship. Then, we both started eating algae.

"Now we have a wonderful strength and calmness between us. Many of the problems of the past several years just aren't considerations any more. We really look forward to our time alone. We didn't have counseling or see a lawyer — we just changed our diet! I never imagined our impending separation was due to a nutritional deficiency!"

Growing up in Fox Lake, Illinois, Suzanne Baldwin relished the cool, delicious well water her family drank, though it stained their sinks and tubs deep orange because of the heavy mineral content. During her first week eating Super Blue Green Algae, she recollected the wonderful well water of her childhood. Mentally, she recalled the thick, alkaline wetness and recognized a familiar gift in this new nourishment. She feels she may have been missing the nutrients she had formerly received from the mineral-rich well water.

"Fifteen years later, my body remembered and blessed this new bounty."

Suzanne Baldwin
Aurora, Illinois

Denise M. Hymans

"For most of my reproductive life, I suffered from bloating, cramping, and mood swings just before and during my menstrual cycle. Over the years, the discomfort and irritability seemed to continue into the month, so that eventually it lasted from one month to the next. I combed the natural foods stores in search of herbs, potions, and vitamins to remedy the situation, to no avail. Three years and countless dollars later, I despaired of finding any help.

"Then I heard about Super Blue Green Algae. The first day I ate some, my oldest child said, 'Hey, Mom! You're in a great mood today!' Only then did I notice that I was, indeed, feeling lighter and brighter. Now every day is better than the one before. That month, my menstrual cycle came and went with no ominous premonition and no discomfort. This change has continued up to the present, and I feel wonderful!

"Previously, my forgetfulness had also begun to concern me. It had become so obvious that my children would tease me about growing senile. Others made excuses for me, 'You're such a busy person, with so much on your mind. No wonder you can't remember anything.' Not wanting to believe that I might have irreversible memory loss or a deteriorating mental condition, I bought the justifications.

"After eating algae for a while, things changed. I no longer put my keys in the refrigerator. I'm not senile after all! My family always observes the changes in me before I can see them myself. Needless to say, my three sons, one husband, four horses, two dogs, two cats, large parrot, rats, and hampsters all eat Super Blue Green Algae. Most of them have algae stories, too.

"Now, at forty-three years young, I can't imagine what my body and mind would be like without my algae."

Denise M. Hymans
Penryn, California

Shawn Kelley

Shawn Kelley felt as if she had the body of a seventy year old. As a checker at a local grocery store, she would spend long hours on her feet rotating her torso, pushing items from one side to the other, and lifting bags and boxes that were too heavy for her. After standing for a few hours, she would experience shooting sensations down her legs and tingling in both hands.

Shawn also endured an assortment of vague and discomfiting complaints for which she ingested ten different prescription medications. She had trouble falling asleep at night, sleeping fitfully even then. Chewing antacids throughout the day was her only relief for a raw, irritated stomach lining and annoying acid reflux. Since childhood, a chronic, pervasive tiredness had kept Shawn from participating in enjoyable activities. Her heavy menstrual cycle (lasting up to nine or ten days each month) would take at least two weeks to recover from because of the extreme blood loss. Her iron count remained low, and so did her energy level. With no motivation to participate in family endeavors, Shawn found sedentary substitutes that often lead to the refrigerator. Seeking to elevate her mood and increase her well-being, she needed extra fuel and empty calories to get her through the day.

Eventually, Shawn began having Network Chiropractic care for the lingering effects of a back injury. Shortly thereafter, at the recommendation of her chiropractor and her therapist, she started eating Super Blue Green Algae. Within a day, her body began to cleanse itself of years worth of toxic buildup in her tissues. As is common when flushing poisons from the body, Shawn initially experienced uncomfortable symptoms. Her head ached intermittently, and bouts of nausea persisted for several months. Within a week, she recalls that "the worst diarrhea I had ever had" sent her to her physician for a stool culture. Finding parasites, he gave her medication which cleared the infection within several weeks. In Shawn's opinion, the parasites had been in her body for many years and may explain some of the debilitating fatigue from which she had suffered since childhood. Because this type of parasite is found in rivers and creeks, Shawn feels that she may have acquired the infection through frequenting local swimming holes.

Though the symptoms Shawn experienced as her body cleansed and replenished itself were often difficult, she emphasizes the rewards of a healthy body that result from this process. Today, she falls asleep easily and sleeps soundly every night. Her energy level has risen dramatically so that she feels "like jumping up and down."

"I have excited butterflies in my stomach all the time, my self-esteem has skyrocketed, and I'm thrilled to be alive. Before, I was existing. Now, I'm living!"

Without the need for empty calories and high carbohydrate snacks, Shawn is making better food choices. Now when she looks in the mirror, she likes what she sees.

This winter was one of the healthiest Shawn has spent in her life. Normally, she would be sick with lung complaints, sore throats, colds, and flu. This year, her only illness came at the end of the season as a mild sinus infection. As a grocery clerk in contact with people and food, this increased health is a bonus for her and her customers. Her menstrual cycle has shortened to a more manageable five or six days of moderate flow, and her iron count remains steady. Her last blood test showed hemoglobin and hematocrit within the normal range. This means she can participate in activities that she hasn't enjoyed since she was a little girl. For the first time in thirty years, she is rollerskating with her children.

Instead of feeling like a seventy year old woman, she now feels twenty. "I feel awesome!" says Shawn. "There are algae eaters, and there are non-algae eaters. I don't want to be part of the latter."

Shawn Kelley
Foresthill, California

Ginny

"I had met Ginny only once, at her daughter's wedding. She seemed frail and full of fear, lacking confidence and direction. We exchanged phone numbers, and late one evening I received a call from her. In a hushed and hesitant tone, she confided in me that she planned to kill herself that night. She had been out of work for some time, she confided, and she couldn't picture herself as a homeless street person. Though we hardly knew each other, she wanted to give me the details of the whereabouts of her personal property, rather than alarm her only daughter. I did my best to encourage her to live that night.

Shari McComb

"Several months went by before she telephoned me again. I was so relieved to hear her voice. 'You know that tape about Super Blue Green Algae you sent me a few months ago?' she inquired. 'I listened to it, and I would like to try the products.' And so she did.

"The next time I saw Ginny, I could not believe my eyes. She had a much stronger appearance; her eyes were bright, her beautiful features seemed more integrated, and she looked clearer. Each day, she set out to find herself a job so that she could leave the welfare roles behind.

"Today, Ginny has a job in a grocery store. Her health has improved, and her daughter enjoys spending time with her. I am encouraging her to share her story and Super Blue Green Algae with everyone she meets. For Ginny, it has been a life-saver."

Shari McComb
Laguna Hills, California

Jason Vance

"I almost died of starvation when I was a year old. After I turned twenty, I developed an inflammatory condition of the large intestine, for which there is no cure.

"Many years later, I began experiencing severe low back pain. Physical therapy didn't help, and pain medication only increased the symptoms. Doctors proposed extensive surgery to remove a vertebral disc and stabilize my spine using metal rods and plates. They not only offered no guarantee that this would alleviate my pain, but they said it was possible that my pain would *increase*. I rejected this option.

"The clinic where I had been employed as a psychotherapist closed. I taught at a college for a year, but had to resign because I couldn't handle the physical and mental stress of teaching. I was plagued with persistent anxiety and frequent depression.

"After I moved into a senior citizens housing project, my pain became so severe that I could stand for only a few minutes. I couldn't walk farther than a block. Life wasn't much fun. Just five years before, I had celebrated my sixtieth birthday with a moonlight skiing party. During that summer I had hiked ten miles a day or more in the mountains. Two years later, that kind of activity was impossible. I became angry that I was forced into a sedentary life. My passion for knowledge through reading was still very satisfying, but the rest of my life was not.

"I took a part-time job with the Forest Service through their senior citizens program. Even the simple tasks my job required left me mentally and physically exhausted after a few hours. Luckily, it was there that I became reacquainted with Tracey, a recreation and wilderness ranger. I had met her once before about ten years earlier. Learning about my health problems, Tracey extolled the merits of Super Blue Green Algae, but I was skeptical, even cynical. I had heard about this product from another friend, Mikala, years before, and had decided

"Jason Vance (right) with friend Alan Peterson. Jason writes, "On June 1st this year, I hiked for ten miles at an elevation of 11,000 feet with no discomfort."

then that my health problems were too severe to be affected by anything as simple as algae.

"Tracey didn't try to sell me anything. I appreciated that. Occasionally, when she saw me limping around the ranger station in pain, she would casually mention the algae. After a few months, in despair and desperation, I asked her for more information. Other Forest Service rangers and employees were also eating algae and reported its positive effects.

"When I learned about the Cell Tech Solution* projects, I became intrigued. I read books and articles and watched videos about Super Blue Green Algae. I also listened to audio tapes about the company and its products, as well as testimonials from people who had benefited from eating this incredible food. At that point, I decided that I had nothing to lose and maybe a lot to gain by including algae in my nutritional program.

"By the end of the year, I started with the EAT kit. In three days, I noticed less fatigue. By day five, I felt a definite increase in energy. Only six days later, I recorded in my journal that I was experiencing less physical pain, and therefore less frustration. My anxiety had decreased. Episodes of depres-

* See page 141 for more information on the Cell Tech Solution.

sion no longer existed. I awoke each morning energetic and alert, and ended each day with vitality to spare. My bowel function became more normal than it had been since the intestinal problem began forty-seven years earlier.

"After only three weeks, I took my first long walk. It was just a mile, but it felt great! As I continued walking each day, I noticed my stride becoming longer and looser. One day, I picked up something that I had dropped on the floor and realized that I had done so without the usual moaning, groaning, and cussing. By the first of the next month, I was riding my exercise bicycle with enthusiasm. I rode 50 minutes (9 miles) the first day, 80 minutes (15 miles) the second day, 85 minutes (16.5 miles) the third day, and 103 minutes (20.5 miles) the fourth day. Since then, I have been working out on it daily. My interests in food have also changed without conscious effort. Fruits and vegetables have become much more appealing than animal products. My body has continued to loosen up, and I can walk two miles with little or no discomfort.

"Years ago, a friend, Mikala, opened a window of opportunity for me and I chose to close it. I regret that now. I missed years of better health and enjoyment of life. Tracey came along and opened that window again. I am very grateful to her for that."

"Postscript: Sonya, my sixteen year old cat, just reminded me to tell you that since she started eating algae, she has also become more active and fit. Many of her health problems have diminished, and her fur is glossier than ever before. She has become very sociable with my friends and visitors."

Jason Vance, M.A.
Durango, Colorado

> "*The animal stories may even be more numerous than the people stories.*"
>
> —Jason Vance

3

Animal Stories

Aphanizomenon flos-aquae exhibit more complex patterns than Spirulina and Chlorella, two strains of artificially cultivated blue-green algae. This indicates that Super Blue Green Algae possesses "greater vibrational fields. . .greater free energy and generative forces. . .a higher consciousness and. . .a higher stage of evolution" than either Spirulina or Chlorella.

—*Optocrystallization Patterns: A Report of the Photographs Showing the Vibrational Properties of Freshwater Algae, 1994. (Available through Cell Tech.)*

Introduction to Animal Stories

Symptoms. Drugs to hide them. More profound symptoms, stronger drugs. Finally, symptoms that can no longer be hidden — then what? Surgery? Acceptance? Reduced capacity and function? Death?

Such can be life in modern medicine. And the same holds true for veterinary medicine. Our pets are suffering from the same diseases that their owners can contract — life-style diseases, earned, not caught. More often than not, these diseases are related to the quality of food our animals consume.

Pets in the wild eat mice, rabbits, deer — all sorts of little creatures. And they eat the whole animal, including enzyme and vitamin rich intestinal contents and partially digested plant materials.

No matter what the advertisements say, we simply cannot replace this type of diet with cooked grains, beans, and synthetic vitamins. We can't even come close!

The result, in my opinion, is that most of our pets are in some way malnourished. Can we feed them wildlife? Of course not. More meat? No, not without destroying the environment at an even greater pace.

The best answer I have found is to add some *wild* to their diet. Wild Aphanizomenon flos-aquae (Super Blue Green Algae) has made huge differences in the health of pets all over North America, as have Cell Tech's other foods that are high in antioxidants and valuable minerals and vitamins.

During my seventeen years in veterinary practice, I couldn't satisfactorily answer the most basic question, "What do I feed my pet to keep it in top health?" Now, I know: Cell Tech products enhance the quality of any diet, and the results have been exciting! It's simple and effective.

Keith Jeffery, DVM
British Columbia, Canada

Sharon Trump

The newly hatched gosling was still wet and exhausted from pecking its way out of the shell. Its mother didn't seem to notice that several large fire ants were crawling all over it. As it lay among the broken remnants of its shell, it peeped pitifully each time it was stung.

Luckily, Sharon happened along. Realizing that fire ants can quickly kill a young gosling, she scooped it up and plucked off the tormenters. As Sharon

The little gosling has grown up.

says, she "hijacked it" and gave it to another more attentive mother. The new mother, Shadow, took the shivering baby immediately under her wing to warm it.

The next morning, the hatchling was still alive, but had developed a runny eye and congested breathing. "Rats!" thought Sharon. "No way am I going to give this little guy antibiotics." She decided to drop a solution of Super Blue Green Algae and water into the gosling's affected eye, so she mixed one Alpha Sun capsule into two ounces of liquid. Sharon also put some on the gosling's bill to help with the congestion. By the next day, he was better.

Sharon remembered Super Blue Green Acidophilus. "This probiotic secretes acidophylline, a natural antibiotic," she thought. She tried a new mixture (one capsule of acidophilus in two ounces of water) in baby's eye and on his nostrils. Some of the algae water dripped off his bill and into his mouth. "Yum!" He wanted more. As Sharon fed him another drop, he tilted his head up to swallow, then dove at the dropper for thirds. . .and fourths. . .and on and on.

The next day, the baby goose appeared to be back to normal and was breathing well. By now, the little fluff ball had captured Sharon's heart. She named him Sweetie. Says Sharon, "I have continued to feed Sweetie from the eye dropper full of algae and acidophilus whenever Shadow brings him into the barn at night. He is eating grass and grain now, but he sure likes his algae toddy at night. He is strong and healthy and growing fast, and he is staying quite tame."

> *"She decided to drop a solution of Super Blue Green Algae and water into the gosling's affected eye. . ."*

*   *   *

Duke is a thirteen year old German shepherd owned by Sharon's neighbor, Annie. Three or four years ago, Duke was shot at close range in the rump with a shotgun. As a result, this previously robust animal has experienced debilitating soreness in his back end, causing him to walk very carefully, with his hips sloped down, as if every step is an extreme effort. Prior to his injury, Duke loved to chase shadows his owner would create for him to pounce on. Now, no more shadow-jumping.

Annie decided to feed him some algae to see if a nutritional approach might give him some relief. The first few days, Duke attempted to eat his dog food and avoid the algae that was sprinkled through it. What was this strange stuff? He even tried snorting it off his dried kibble. After a few days, he apparently realized that this weird green powder was helping him feel better. Not only did he finish every crumb in his bowl, but he begged for more!

One day, Sharon and her friend Bev came to visit Annie

and her energetic pooch. Duke ran over to greet them, sniffed at Bev's purse, and looked up at them expectantly. He followed them around incessantly and continued nudging Bev's handbag until he finally got her attention. "What could he possibly want in my purse?" she wondered. Looking inside, she discovered a small container of animal algae that she had forgotten. Annie had run out of her supply that day, so Duke had gone without it. Bev generously spooned several tablespoons into his food bowl. Gulp! It was gone. Duke begged for more, so she gave it to him. Gulp! It, too, was gone!

On closer inspection, Sharon noticed a weeping lesion on Duke's hind quarters in the same area as the gunshot wound. She surmised that this may have been a detoxification of the old injury. Annie lamented that it was nearly impossible to keep salve or a dressing on this sore because Duke would either lick it off or it would slide off with the blood and ooze. Always a quick thinker, Sharon poured some animal algae onto the open wound while Duke was busy devouring his third helping. Then they went inside the house to visit.

An hour later, when the ladies emerged to check on Duke, he was considerably better: his eyes appeared brighter and clearer, and he was ready to play. He even wanted to jump on shadows! The weeping sore had coagulated into a soft scab.

To keep Duke from licking the algae off his hip, Annie devised a piece of doggie clothing that worked. She cut a hole into a pair of women's bikini pants for Duke's tail and slipped them on over his rump. One day, after canvassing the neighborhood in his fancy bikinis, Duke came home, ate his food and algae concoction, and then disappeared for four days. Annie and Sharon frantically called the dog pound and then began checking around town. Finally, they found him. Rascally Duke had set up camp at the home of a neighbor whose female dog had just come into heat. Naturally, he had slipped off his underwear for his rendezvous.

Once home, he should have been ready for a hearty meal. When Annie placed his food dish in front of him, Duke sat on his haunches and stared at it. Then he looked imploringly up at his mistress, as if to say, "Are we forgetting something?"

As soon as Annie mixed in his algae, he jumped up and gobbled down his dinner.

Atta' boy, Duke!

*   *   *

Sharon does love her horses! She has two thoroughbreds that were raised for the race track many years ago. Now, at sixteen and seventeen, they have become family pets. Because Sharon had always fed them well, she did not expect to see much difference when she added Super Blue Green Algae to their diets. Within two weeks, however, they had changed dramatically. They began to act like young foals, playing hard and inventing games.

One of their favorite tricks seems to be taking the lids off garbage cans to root around for discarded goodies. Another annoying habit they have formulated is helping to unload packages from the trunk of the car. Unfortunately, they often eat the groceries. One day when the phone rang, they each consumed an

Vader and friend Tiger warily watch Sharon snap their picture.

entire loaf of bread before Sharon could run back out to the car to retrieve her shopping.

One of the horses, Vader, used to be less sociable than the other. He was more of a horse's horse. To him, people were for providing food, but that was it. Since he's been eating algae regularly, his temperament has changed. He's much more affectionate, following along after his owners and nuzzling them with his nose. Vader has mellowed so much that he is now a joy to ride. Before the algae, there were times when he would rear and bolt suddenly. He is seventeen hands tall and extremely powerful, so this tactic scared Sharon. Now he begs to go for his ride and craves attention.

After feeding the horses algae for six months, Sharon noticed that their coats glowed. They were vibrant! Their hooves used to be plagued with fungus problems from the damp Florida earth, with recurring cracks, tender soles, and abscesses. None of the supplements Sharon had previously tried for these problems made any difference. In fact, some had caused Vader to develop *founder* symptoms.* Since beginning the algae, however, their hooves are stronger and grow at a much faster rate, with no more wall separations or infections.

On occasion, Sharon comes out to feed her beloved horses in the evening and discovers she has forgotten their algae. As she dashes back to the house to fetch it, Vader follows close behind to supervise the operation, waiting just outside the open door for her to retrieve the jar from the cupboard. He is so bold now that Sharon thinks that if she didn't bring his special algae out immediately, he'd probably come right in and get it!

Sharon Trump
Orlando, Florida

---

* Please see "Lady" beginning on page 135 to learn more about symptoms of founder.

Waldo the Wonderful

"Vance! Come and get your algae," called his wife. As usual, she counted out his acidophilus, enzymes, Omega Sun, Alpha Sun, and Sprouts and Algae tablets into a small dish and set it on a tray on the kitchen counter. Vance glanced at his watch. Oh, oh. Running late. He'd have to eat his algae when he got home from work that evening.

> "*Never leave your algae out where the cats can get it.*"

Late in the day, after appointments and meetings, Vance pulled into his driveway. Waldo, the fluffy, black and white feline member of the family, waited patiently at the front door for his master to let him in. Whew! What a day. They were both glad to be home. Vance removed his shoes in the hall and padded into his den to check his messages. Crash! Something fell to the floor in the kitchen. "What has Waldo knocked over now?" he wondered.

By the time Vance made it to the kitchen, wily Waldo had devoured the capsules and was chomping contentedly on the algae tablets. As he munched eagerly, the finicky feline gingerly extended one paw to grope for a tablet that had rolled across the floor. He couldn't tear himself away from his delicious snack to fetch it properly.

Poor Vance had to do without his algae that day, but Waldo's feelin' fine!

Vance Storrs
Auburn, California

Peaches, Pebbles, and Bob

Another "Gulp! I can't believe I ate the whole thing!" story.

Chris Nunes, a new algae eater in Paso Robles, California, ordered a box of BG Bites from Cell Tech. Several days later, the UPS truck pulled up to her house and the delivery driver left her package at the front door. Unbeknownst to him, Chris's very large, very hungry dogs had free run of her yard. By the time Chris arrived home from work, Peaches, Pebbles, and Bob had consumed the entire box of snacks, including the wrappers! Fortunately, they suffered no ill-effects from their first "unauthorized algae feast," but Chris did notice that they exhibited an unusual amount of energy that evening.

To Cell Tech's credit, when Chris called Distributor Services to recount her tale (or tail) of woe, the representative apologized for the inconvenience and offered to send a replacement. "It might take a week or two, though," she cautioned. Two days later, a shipment from Cell Tech arrived by second day air containing not only the box of BG Bites, but two complimentary tapes and a *New Leaf* magazine! Chris was impressed. What great service!

Kathryn Reid-Carriero
Auburn, California

Topper

"Orange cats are most unique. . .ours came to us as an adult. My oldest son's former girlfriend called in tears one day asking if we would please take her beloved cat. A year before, her parents had filed for divorce. The four-legged family members had been sorted out and as-signed new lives. The young woman had

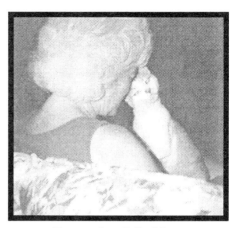

Topper gives Polly Meyers some friendly nuzzling.

come home from school one day to find her horse, the love of her life, gone! Her mother had secretly sold him and the new owners had trailered him away that day. Due to economics, she, her mother, and her brother were to move to an apart-ment. Now Topper, the orange cat, must go, too.

"Topper is a lover. He nibbles your chin, gently touching your cheeks and lips with his paws, insisting on sharing his affection equally with anyone close by.

"Unfortunately, Topper regularly lost huge chunks of hair, leaving sticky, oozing sores where the hair had once been. We suspected that he was allergic to flea bites. Then, when he was about ten years old, he developed numerous scabs on his nose and ears and one large wound in the corner of his eye. This one was of particular concern, because it never healed, regardless of the treatment we offered. If the scab was knocked off, the sore would bleed profusely for a long time.

"When I started taking the algae, the lesion had been in the corner of Topper's eye for over a year and a half. I put some algae on his wet food, but Topper chose to dine exclusively on his dry cat chow. Frustrated that he had rejected his algae-laced meal, I decided to slip one Alpha Sun and one Omega Sun tablet down his throat each morning. On the tenth day, I came home from work to find that the scab had fallen off. No blood! The next day, the crust had reformed. Several months went by and the scab fell off repeatedly, replaced each time by a slightly smaller one. It has been over a year now since the last occurrence. Scar tissue remains and no hair grows on that spot. A quarter inch wide hole at the corner of his eye reminds us of what used to be.

"Topper's hair falls out less often now. I comb him regularly to keep the fleas at bay and when he does get a bite, the reaction is much less severe.

"Topper still plays like a kitten, running, chasing, and playing soccer with his ball. If he does something wrong and I verbally reprimand him as I put him outside, several hours later I will hear a special kind of cry, and I know he has brought me a present of apology. He'll drop a mouse or a gopher at my feet and refuse to eat it until I have told him what a good kitty he is and that everything is okay. Life is good when you have friends like that."

Polly Meyers
Ramona, California

Valentine

Valentine is a two year old, ninety pound German shepherd born on February 14th. Last year she was a Search and Rescue dog on the Connecticut Search Team, which is also when she and her owner, Frank, began eating Super Blue Green Algae.

According to Frank, he had been giving Valentine two Alpha Sun and one enzyme capsule each morning for two weeks when he noticed a change in her appearance. Her coat looked shinier, and her digestion seemed to be functioning better. Since puppyhood, Valentine had frequently eaten great quantities of grass, and nothing Frank did to discourage her made any difference. Now that she eats algae, she no longer searches for additional chlorophyll by grazing outside. With sweeter smelling breath as a pleasant side effect, Valentine doesn't even smell like a dog. (Like roses, maybe?)

Frank and Valentine both seem to sleep more deeply since they began eating Super Blue Green Algae, and they wake more alert and ready to go. For Search and Rescue dogs, work is play, and it used to be that when Valentine wasn't working, she would laze about. The algae has given her so much energy that she now frolics even when she isn't working.

Frank has also seen an increase in her stamina and endurance in the field. In the past, he watched her closely to make sure that she had a break and a snack when she seemed tired. Recently, Frank did a two hour training with Valentine in Bushnell Park, which is approximately eight acres of numerous trees and expansive open areas.

Although Valentine can pick up a scent on the ground, her specialty is primarily tracking air scent. On this day, the training in question involved an exercise to teach her to locate people in trees, which meant Valentine was learning to look upward as soon she caught a scent. (Apparently, lost people often do peculiar things such as climbing trees, digging themselves into holes, or burying themselves.) The trainers conducted the lesson during the lunch hour, with many people present, so that she would really have to work the scent. When Valentine finally discovered Frank's partner in a tree, she became so excited that she ran to Frank with her tail wagging, full of energy and pep, as if she had "little springs in her feet." Previously, she might have sauntered tiredly over to Frank, tongue lolling out, obviously needing a rest.

> *"The algae has given her so much energy that she now frolics even when she isn't working."*

Valentine's owner is monitoring his resourceful pooch by charting her energy and activity levels during the day. He has noticed that she eats less, and he's curious to find out if she is getting more value from her food because she is using it more efficiently. Frank says, "If one half of what is happening in me is happening in her, I'm thrilled!"

Carol Bennett
Durango, Colorado

A note from Carol Bennett:

"The above story appeared in its original form in *Spirit Symbols Animal Connection Network Newstestament*, Vol. 2, Issue 1. As the editor of this publication and founder of the Animal Connection Network, I have collected thousands of stories over the past three years from pet professionals and pet owners. My own experience with Super Blue Green Algae for myself and my animals led me to search for better health answers for all of us. From the number of positive stories people have told me about their animals and Super Blue Green Algae, I feel that this wild, natural food is indeed intended for all life."

Lady

"Joe! Come quickly!" exclaimed Kathy. "Lady's down and can hardly walk at all." The phone call came early in the morning before farrier Joe Elliott left for work.

Lady's owner, Kathy, had telephoned her veterinarian earlier when she noticed that her horse was having great difficulty walking. She lay down frequently and appeared to be in agony. After x-raying Lady's hooves, the vet diagnosed the condition as an inflammation of the lamina called *founder*.

When the experienced farrier examined Lady, he noticed a cresty roll of tissue on the top of her neck. Joe has observed this to be an early warning sign of founder, which he believes results from an overly rich diet. Too much of a good thing, such as high-protein alfalfa (actually meant as cattle feed) or large quantities of grain can quickly bring on this disorder. Toxic residues travel throughout the body and finally to the hooves, causing them to become so hot and tender that any movement can be excruciating. The ensuing decrease in circulation to the extremities results in areas of bruising and soft spongy soles. The normally hard consistency of the outer hooves becomes crumbly and difficult to shoe. Additionally, the toxins begin to destroy the lamina which holds the coffin bone in place. This bone can then rotate, and eventually could even pierce the sole. Without healthy feet, the horse is unable to walk or stand, and may have to be euthanized. As they say in the horse world, "No foot, no horse!"

Lady's x-ray showed that her coffin bones were rotated approximately twelve degrees. As part of the treatment, Kathy's vet recommended special shoes for the affected feet which would help support and cushion the hooves, perhaps allowing them to return to normal.

Joe knew exactly which shoes to use. But poor Lady! She was in so much discomfort that Joe was unable to work on one foot longer than a minute or two before letting her rest. Then he'd work on the other foot briefly and allow her to rest again. A normal shoeing job takes one hour for four feet. In Lady's case, it took two hours for just the front two feet. One hour per hoof!

Because hooves grow very slowly, changes occur gradually. With a foundered horse, it might take six months to a year before the damaged tissue extends far enough to trim away the distortion and leave a healthy hoof in its place. Usually, at least three shoeing cycles six to eight weeks apart must transpire for any substantial improvement to appear.

Joe and his wife, Cindy, had recently begun eating a wild-grown nutritional product called Super Blue Green Algae that contains a broad range of minerals and amino acids. They were very pleased with their results. Just that week, Joe had listened to a tape in which a respected Texas veterinarian had described some of the excellent changes her clients had experienced. One foundered horse had improved substantially within only one shoeing cycle! This doctor explained that just as our nails require minerals and proteins to grow healthy and strong, so do the fur and "nails" of animals.

While Joe remained skeptical, he hoped that Super Blue Green Algae would benefit his clientele in a similar fashion. Lady was his first opportunity, so he recommended it to Kathy and scheduled a reexamination in seven weeks.

When he returned for Lady's appointment, Joe was amazed to find that enough of the new hoof had grown back for him to trim away most of the bruised and traumatized tissue so that he could shoe her normally. A comparative x-ray was taken which showed that the previously rotated coffin bones had improved significantly. Best of all, Lady seemed free of discomfort and almost completely back to normal. As Joe watched her trot happily around the area, tossing her mane and tail, he noticed that she limped slightly on the curves but seemed a hundred percent sound on the straight away.

One week later, Kathy called Joe to tell him that her horse was running around the corral, bucking and frolicking like a young colt. "I'm supposed to go to my annual horse camp in the mountains next week with my friends. Do you think Lady will be well enough?" she wondered. Joe cautioned her to take it easy at first and keep an eye on her horse, but to go ahead.

According to Cindy Elliott, Kathy and Lady spent most of that summer high in the Cuyumaca mountains as "riding buddies" again without further incident.

Joe and Cindy Elliott
Ramona, California

As an addendum to this story, Joe has continued to shoe this horse every seven weeks. During an examination the following spring, he noticed that Lady's hooves had begun to deteriorate again. They were a little crumbly and difficult to shoe. "Are you still feeding Lady her Super Blue Green Algae?" he asked. Embarrassed, Kathy shook her head and listed some other supplements she had substituted. Of course, Joe recommended immediately resuming algae and stressed the importance of maintaining her horse on this nutrient dense food.

*   *   *

Animals require appropriate building blocks for healthy tissues and organs just as humans do. Unfortunately, they are unable to communicate with us when they hurt or need something we aren't giving them. We may not notice that something is lacking until it presents itself in obvious deficiencies. The best advice from animal care people and veterinarians is to provide our pets with the highest quality feed available, and then add Super Blue Green Algae to it. The food we feed our animals is as depleted as our own, but because theirs is so heavily processed, it may contain even fewer nutrients than ours. Toxic, chemical preservatives are often added to increase shelf life, and the resulting concoction might be not only inedible but harmful.

Hopefully, Lady will receive the care she needs in the form of digestible, chemical-free nutrients, instead of being loved to death with rich feed. We and our animals have the potential to be the best we can be when we eat a sensible diet of whole, organic foods, in as natural a state as possible.

Tigger

"Tigger's story is the reason for this anthology, not because it is unusual or stupendous, but because it sparked an idea.

"We have three cats in our family, and Tigger is the middle one. Like his older brother, he is a domestic shorthair, with orange tabby markings and a furry, white chest. Unlike his siblings, Tigger maintains an independent streak that often gets him into trouble. He frequently wanders home late in the evening after being out all day, and sometimes carries multiple battle scars from unfriendly encounters. More than once, Tigger has acquired an ugly, oozing wound in a cat fight.

"Even though I follow the natural healing model in my chiropractic practice and with my children, in the past I have relied on prescribed medication to combat infections in our animals. One of our other cats even endured the surgical insertion of a drain for several weeks in addition to antibiotic therapy. Whatever the procedure, from injecting pills down his throat to spraying him for fleas, Tigger has never been a willing participant. Peachy and Harley put up with anything as long as it is given with love. Tigger struggles, meows, and claws violently until he is freed from the torture at hand.

"One morning, I noticed Tigger limping when I opened the door to let him in the house. His right forepaw seemed swollen and hot, a sure sign that another abscess had formed. As I held him in my lap and watched him lick the wound, I felt increasingly frustrated at the thought of another round of antibiotics.

" 'How can I do to you what I wouldn't do to my children?' I wondered. And then I began to think about how I would handle this situation if it *were* one of my children.

" 'What is a natural antibacterial agent?' I asked myself.

" 'Tea tree oil,' I thought.

" 'Okay, how could I apply tea tree oil without it stinging too much?'

"I decided to mix the oil with a cup of warm water and place Tigger's paw in it. As his paw encountered the solution, it still must have stung because he began his usual routine of meow, struggle, and claw. Very calmly, I explained to the wiggler how much I loved him and wanted to help him. 'I know it hurts, but I don't want to give you antibiotics and you have to help me help you,' I said soothingly. I felt Tigger's body begin to unwind and relax as I stroked him and talked to him. Before long, he allowed me to hold his paw in the mixture for a minute or so, and when I took it out, he reached up to my neck to nuzzle his head under my chin. It was as if he thanked me for caring enough to help him.

"I knew that Super Blue Green Algae would provide important nutrients for cellular rejuvenation, and I hadn't been giving it to the cats on a regular basis. How could I ensure that Tigger would eat enough to give him the boost he needed? Perhaps if I put it on his leg, he would lick it off as he continued to wash the wound. So I did.

"I sprinkled a small amount of algae on Tigger's paw, which he promptly licked off. I put more on, and he licked that off, too. Hoping he would eat thirds, I put a small pile of the powder on the floor next to his foot. Very quickly, he gobbled that up and looked around for another helping. Over the course of the next few days, I continued to bathe Tigger's paw in the tea tree oil solution and gave him little mounds of algae on the floor.

"After three days, Tigger's swollen foot began to shrink, the heat left, and the sore stopped oozing. At this point, Tigger sniffed his algae pile, tossed his head and walked off. My impression was that he no longer needed such a concentration of nutrients.

"Since then, I mix the Super Blue Green Algae with the cats' dry food, which is available to them at all times. I want them to have the best possible nutrition so that they will live long and healthy lives free of infirmity and disease.

"There is also a side note about our oldest cat, Peachy, who has mellowed considerably with age. I could tell the algae was having an effect on his well-being when he took a flying leap across the kitchen and landed in my lap as I talked on the phone one day. (Peachy is a fifteen pound, twelve year old tomcat who usually pulled himself up into my lap rather slowly and deliberately.) Later on that same day, my daughter and I were in the bedroom when Peachy came tearing down the hall, jumped on the cedar chest, leaped over to the bed, and landed on the desk. 'Mom!' exclaimed my daughter, 'I think you're giving him too much algae!'

"Even animals can feel energetic, lively, and youthful again when they receive all the nutrients they need."

Lisa C. Moore, DC
Auburn, California

4

The Cell Tech Solution

"Your body is not separate from the body of the universe, because at quantum mechanical levels there are no well-defined edges."

— *From the book The Seven Spiritual Laws of Success* © *1994 Deepak Chopra. Reprinted by permission of Amber-Allen Publishing, Inc. P.O. Box 6657, San Rafael, CA 94903. All rights reserved.*

The Cell Tech Solution

Beginning in 1992, Cell Tech earmarked 10% of the yearly algae harvest for people who have the greatest need and the fewest resources. Groups and organizations in many parts of the world now receive algae from Cell Tech as part of rehabilitative nutritional programs for the people they serve. Projects are initially developed by groups of enterprising Cell Tech distributors and are often later sponsored by the company as part of the Cell Tech Solution. In an effort that reaches from California to Cambodia, Cell Tech is dedicated to bringing improved nutrition, and therefore more opportunity, into the lives of the people of the world.

One of the first programs to distribute algae to a group of needy people began with a project in Nicaragua sponsored by the Distributor Empowerment Team in Quebec City, Canada.

Not long after, a noted humanitarian, Naomi Bronstein, began providing desperately needed shelter, food, health care, and education to orphaned, abandoned, abused, disabled, or otherwise disadvantaged children of Cambodia. She also cares for single-parent families and elderly survivors of the twenty-five years of war and holocaust in Southeast Asia. Cell Tech has joined hands with Naomi to provide algae to residents at her Children's Center in Phnom Penh, Cambodia.

Jeanne Kidd saw heartache and poverty in the Dominican Republic and took the algae to needy individuals in that country.

Michael Linden coordinates a program which now supplies infants, teenagers, and indigent people with a constant supply of Super Blue Green Algae.

In the United States, Michael Stewart became involved with a project in inner city Los Angeles. Cell Tech has since become a sponsor of the Hope L.A. Horticulture Corps. Here, teenagers from underprivileged neighborhoods come together to work a two acre plot where drive-by shootings occur regularly.

At the American Indian Family Healing Center in Oakland, California, the staff and residential family receive a daily nutrition program of Super Blue Green Algae. This project represents a successful model that can be expanded to other American Indian Healing Centers.

The Network of Hope is comprised of a group of distributors from around the country who provide algae to learning disabled children.

The Cell Tech Solution is especially dear to the heart of Marta Kollman. While both she and Daryl have a deep love for the children of the world, Marta has been a catalyst for the perpetuation of the Cell Tech Solution projects and the formation of the Cell Tech Solution Fund, which provides monetary support for ancillary services. With this program of sharing and caring, Cell Tech is reaching out the window of opportunity to help people in need, stemming the global tide of poverty and malnutrition.

The following stories are just a sampling of some of the good work being done under the umbrella of the Cell Tech Solution program.

Amigos Para Siempre: "Friends for Always"

In Nandaime, Nicaragua, the doctor handed the listless infant to its mother with a bewildered sigh. Shaking his head, he said, "Take him home from the hospital; there is no hope. Just spend time with him and make him comfortable." In the doctor's opinion, the feverish, semicomatose boy with the red and swollen leg would only survive a few days. He was sorry, but there was nothing he could do.

Marie Claude Simard with a Nicaraguan child.

Marie Claude, a French-Canadian acupuncturist and humanitarian, would not give up so easily. Her mission in Nicaragua was to provide medical care, love, and support for these destitute, poverty stricken families. This included supervising the distribution of the Super Blue Green Algae, donated by herself and the rest of the individuals who comprise the Quebec Distributor Empowerment Team.

The determined woman mixed algae with water in the dying infant's baby bottle and offered it to him at regular intervals. After four or five hours, a spark of life returned to his half-closed, glassy eyes. Slowly, he began to perk up, like a faded flower returning to bloom. Padré Santiago, their priest and protector for eight or nine years, could hardly believe his eyes. He knew then that all the children of Nandaime should have this wonderful, life-giving food.

Marie Claude and the others in the Quebec Distributor Empowerment Team appealed to Marta Kollman and Cell Tech to officially sponsor the Nicaragua project. Marta had wanted to reach out to others less fortunate for some time, and as always, her husband Daryl reserved a special place in his heart for the children of the world. Between the two of them, they answered a hearty *yes!* and the first Cell Tech Solution project was born. A program that began by feeding five hundred youngsters has grown to provide algae for first 1,500, then 3,600 men, women, and children. Since then, the group has stabilized at about 3,000 individuals.

Thirty thousand people live in the city of Nandaime, fifteen thousand in the outskirts, or *barrio*. Their one or two room huts are usually made of bamboo sticks with earthen floors. Six to eight people share these humble quarters, many of them children. Water on the property is often heavily polluted, suitable only for washing clothes or muddy fingers. A family might have a chicken or two scratching in the dust, or if they

Marie Claude Simard and her assistant
prepare nutrient-rich algae for the children.

are very fortunate, a pig. One or two chairs and possibly a table are usually the only furniture in the house. There is often a small pit to make a fire, but no built-in stove or running water. According to Gilles Arbour, member of the Quebec Distributor Empowerment Team, "A typical meal consists of white rice and black beans. The next day, they would probably have black beans and white rice. After that, maybe a tortilla with beans and rice."

Nutritional knowledge is minimal. Most people think vegetables are "not real food." Apparently, only beans and rice are considered "real food," and vegetables are far too expensive for the average family anyway.

The situation is quite different out in the jungle. Here, thousands of people who fled from the war in the northern part of Nicaragua have made a fresh start. "Dumped" there originally, these refugees floundered until they learned to adapt their farming ways to their new land. Now, they have planted bananas, tomatoes, cucumbers, and other crops. They have dug wells and built new homes for themselves. One hot meal a day is provided for them at small kitchens that serve approximately twenty-five people each. It is with these daily rations that some of them are given a serving of Super Blue Green Algae.

Most of the Nandaime algae project is supervised by a community center in town. A group of teenagers is in charge of the algae distribution. When the Quebec team visited this center originally, they found young people with a vacant look in their eyes. They had no future, no goals, and no hope. Since eating the algae and watching their people recapture their energy and spirit, these youngsters have acquired a new zest for life. Among other services that assist the villagers, Manuel, Yessenia, and their coworkers deliver the powdered algae to a school where it's mixed with juice to give to children with a mid-morning snack. During the summer, they travel to individual homes with bottles of algae and specific instructions for its consumption. Two or three nutritionists are now on hand to offer advice and guidance. Padré Guydo Cloutier has joined Padré Santiago in serving the Nandaime people. And, of course, the indomitable Marie Claude, who spends four months a year in Nicaragua, provides homeopathic and naturopathic expertise, and acupuncture when needed.

Sales of the "Nicaragua Report," compiled by John Mann, Gilles Arbour, and Nyrma Hernandez, have generated over $40,000 to fund agricultural assistance and purchase tools. The initial $20,000 purchased a piece of property to create an organic farm, and the remainder will provide money to dig a well and begin the preparation of the land. Fifty people from the center have gravitated to the farm project, and, against compelling odds, find a way to travel there daily to work. Buses are usually late and often break down before they arrive. But these people have hope. They have control over their lives again and their personal power has been restored.

When Padré Santiago sent a letter to the Quebec Distributor Empowerment Team after one month asking for more algae, the project began to grow. His descriptions of the children as having more energy, being more lively, and having bigger smiles captured the hearts of their Canadian friends. He reported that diarrhea, the number one cause of infant mortality in developing countries, was much less severe in the children eating the algae. To save even one child in this manner was a monumental accomplishment. How could the distributors in Quebec City say *No?*

Gilles muses, "When I think of Nicaragua, the first thing that comes to my mind is children: lots of children, smiling, happy, even though they have very little. That's quite a lesson for most of us. The people we work with are the poorest of the poor, but they smile more than my neighbors here. They share anything they have. We've lost a lot of humanness, and *they* have that."

It seems the members of the Quebec Distributor Empowerment Team recaptured some of that "humanness" as they reached out and touched their neighbors to the south.

Gilles Arbour
Quebec, Canada

The Children of Nandaime

Les enfants de Nicaragua. Marie Claude's children. Several times a year this dedicated acupuncturist from Quebec City travels to the barrios of Nandaime, Nicaragua to check up on "her" children. Through the *Centro Comunitario* (Community Center), she administers medical care, algae, and love to the poorest of the poor. She also participates in their nu-

Children receiving algae as part of the Nicaraguan Project.

tritional education. In addition to dispensing algae, she has taught them to grow different kinds of sprouts to supplement their meager diets. Marie Claude states emphatically that these two foods have made a measurable difference in the health of the people she serves.

Young ones from many different sectors of Nandaime are drawn to the Centro Comunitario in search of employment and food. Here, they have the opportunity to work on the youth farm, receiving two hot meals and a daily dose of algae capsules.

While the work among the *colectivo de trabajo* on the farm can be physically demanding, the participants join in willingly and with enthusiasm as their energy levels remain constant. Wholesome meals, life-giving sprouted grains, and Super Blue Green Algae provide them with the nourishment they need. Marie Claude shares several examples of children who have benefited from this combination.

*   *   *

Jimmy, a sixteen year old boy from a very poor family, was a sickly, underweight young man with no energy and no motivation. Before joining the Community Center he lived with his grandmother, but because he needed money to pay for school materials and medicines, he began working at the youth farm in the mornings, attending school in the afternoons, and studying his lessons at night.

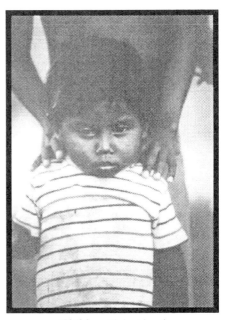

Child participating in the algae feeding program.

Very quickly, Jimmy noticed his attention span increasing and his energy level rising. He no longer fell asleep at his desk, he participated in school dances, and he even had enough strength to join the baseball club. Previously, Jimmy suffered from frequent colds and flu, but with his new diet, his health has improved greatly.

At the end of each month, the *Clinica-Farmacia Naturalista IXCHEL,* sponsored by the Centro Comunitario, weigh the participants in the "alternative nutrition" program. Marie Claude says that although Jimmy worked harder and longer than ever before, engaged in many after-school sports, studied at night, and attended school in the afternoons, he actually gained weight on this regimen. In his words, "Algae makes all the difference!"

*   *   *

Twelve year old Erick and his eleven year old brother lived on the streets of Nandaime after their father left for Costa Rica and their mother abandoned them. Occasionally, they would appeal to their grandmother for food and a roof over their heads, but mostly they fended for themselves. Some time ago, Erick came to the Centro Comunitario looking for employment and food. He had been working in the sugar cane fields, but preferred the idea of the youth farm, where he would receive, in his words, "Two meals a day and vitamins" (algae).

Twice daily, Erick consumes his hot meals and his algae. According to Marie Claude, "He has not been ill since his arrival, has gained weight, and his skin condition has disappeared." He puts in long hours at the youth farm, performs well in school, and is now learning folkloric dances. Recently, Erick brought his underweight little brother, weighing only seventy-five pounds, to join the program.

*   *   *

Nineteen year old Eliezer ("Chino") is in his first year at a local agricultural college. Just a year ago, he performed so poorly in school that he was in danger of failing his examination for high school graduation. Malaria, fevers, and other health problems plagued him, and he fell asleep during his classes on a regular basis.

Since joining the program at the center, Chino has "pulled his socks up" to complete his twelfth grade examination and has gone on to college in Rivas, Nicaragua. Although he has not gained any weight with his improved nutrition, Chino has developed into a tall, healthy young man.

*   *   *

Little Louisa lived in Monte Grande near the youth farm. Seven years old, undersized, and weak from the draining effects of a parasitic infection, she came to the farm to have the *"pastila de vitamina"* (algae capsules) with the youth workers at their morning break. Now that her health has improved, she works two hours a day, receives algae and *ajonjoli* (sesame butter) on a slice of bread, and requests more chores. With this work, she earns enough money to pay for the preschool she attends in the afternoons, as well as extra money for her basic supplies. In addition to her renewed vibrant health, and because of her pastila de vitamina, Louisa's happy laugh has returned and she has energy to spare.

*   *   *

At thirteen years old, Juan Carlos started school very late because of a disfiguring, itchy skin disease. His mother had tried different types of lotions, but because they were poor, they could not afford anything better. Juan's social life dwindled because of the shame he carried over his pockmarked face. After joining the Centro, he began working with the "rabbit gang" (a group that cares for the farm's rabbits), eating his sprouts and his algae every day. Soon, he noticed an improvement in his health.

Within several weeks, his skin condition vanished completely, he gained weight, and he began to feel much better about himself. Marie Claude reports that Juan Carlos now "assists the kindergarten children in the Modesto barrio during his spare time and performs well in school. He joined the junior baseball team, works in the rabbit program regularly, and teaches his mother about sprouting grains (beans, sesame, and corn)."

Marie Claude sees many examples of the miracle of Super Blue Green Algae during her trips to Nandaime. When she asks the children how they like their algae, they all show her their Superhero muscles "just like Superman!" The only complaints she hears come from the exhausted mothers whose active children now have so much energy that they keep their poor parents on the run. If they, too, received Super Blue Green Algae, they would have no problem!

Marie Claude expresses her appreciation to Cell Tech and the Cell Tech Solution, "All our gratefulness to Cell Tech for their help."

Marie Claude Simard
Quebec, Canada

Republica Dominica

The Dominican Republic shares the Caribbean island of Hispaniola with the country of Haiti. At one time, it served as an intermediate harbor for the importation of slaves. While a few families retain their pure European or African heritage, most Haitians are a blend of French and West African, and the Dominicans are mainly an African and Spanish mix. Regardless of lineage, most of the population of this semitropical island tend to be poor and unemployed.

In 1992, Jeanne Marie Kidd and her husband traveled to the Dominican Republic with their six month old daughter, Kelley, as part of a mission group to help children. They knew they would find a country desperately in need of their help, but what greeted them far exceeded their expectations. Their plane landed in the capital city of Santo Domingo, now the most modern city in the Caribbean, which is also the oldest European settlement in the New World. As they drove down the crowded streets, they saw people on bicycles with children riding on the handle bars or in baskets. Mangled hands and feet testified to the mishaps that often result from this kind of transportation. Most of the people on the island are generally too poor to afford an automobile, or even a motorcycle.

The countryside consists of shanty towns with humble, one-room huts made of corrugated iron panels, or cinder block walls and thatched roofs. With little regard for marriage, many men in Santo Domingo father many children with a variety of women, which results in large families living in cramped quarters. Without much incentive to work, and the limited income that follows, Dominican men have numerous mouths to feed and not many resources to draw upon.

A large percentage of these children also need medical care. Jeanne deciphered the Spanish language charts on the walls of clinics and doctors' offices. They recommended weaning babies onto infant formula quickly, then giving them solid food by three or four months. Because the families are so destitute, mothers purchase the formula and then dilute it with water to make it last longer. Unfortunately, the water usually contains harmful intestinal parasites. In addition, the people think it prudent to add great quantities of sugar to this concoction. Not only are the children not receiving the full compliment of nutrients from their formula, but the sugar undoubtedly affects their immune function as well. The dental consequences keep the local dentists busy.

It was in the waiting room of the mission's dentist that Jeanne observed the only other woman she saw who, like herself, nursed an older child. This nine-month old baby was the one Dominican infant that resembled Kelley in size and general health. Other children twice her daughter's age were half as big.

Jeanne's translator, Anita, also commented on the discrepancy between Kelley's health and that of the local *bambinos*. Jeanne had become a Cell Tech distributor a year and a half before, and she explained to Anita that her baby had the added benefit of nutrients from the algae through her breast milk. Six months later, when Anita returned to the United States, she, too, signed up with Cell Tech.

Although Jeanne had no personal connection with the Dominican people, her heart went out to all the children who would never have the chance to grow up as healthy and strong as her own little girl. "Wouldn't it be great to find a way for these kids to have algae, too?" she thought wistfully.

That summer, at the August Celebration, Jeanne heard Gilles Arbour describe a new project in Nicaragua that provided Super Blue Green Algae to a group of malnourished children. Moved to tears, she vowed to Daryl Kollman that she would begin a similar program in the Dominican Republic.

Through Anita, Jeanne heard about an orphanage in the Neyba valley, in the southwest section of the country, that clothed, fed, and housed twenty-four children. "Would Fernando, the director of the facility, be interested in having Super Blue Green Algae supplied to all of these children?"

wondered Jeanne. She and Anita asked him.

"I would be honored," he replied.

With the financial help of the Knoxville Distributor Empowerment Team and many other individuals, after one and a half years of concerted effort, the initial project emerged.* The first shipment arrived in the Dominican Republic in September 1994. It included enough algae, acidophilus, bifidus, and money for parasite medication for all the children in the orphanage. During this time, Jeanne approached Cell Tech to assume the Dominican project as part of the Cell Tech Solution. She was originally told that this transfer could occur once the operation had been in place for six months. Unfortunately, this time frame coincided with a cycle of particularly rapid growth for the company. Unprepared for this massive phenomenon, Cell Tech's home office required all available resources to accommodate the changes. The Dominican project would have to wait.

A desperate Jeanne appealed to Cell Tech distributors for their assistance. She requested money rather than algae because of the substantial discount available for large orders. In addition, she calculated the distributor percentage on each order and returned this amount to the project account. Amazingly, she received fifty responses to her plea for help and was able to carry the program until Cell Tech embraced it in September of 1995. The Neyba orphanage and the first grade of a local school are now official Cell Tech Solution projects. This means they receive all the algae they need directly from Cell Tech.

Jeanne tells how their ongoing fund also provides additional materials for the local school in Neyba. The school receives subsides from another organization in the United States, but Jeanne has taken it upon herself to send additional items to these children, who had no school building and sat upon rocks instead of chairs. Imagine the level of poverty required for a person to feel excitement and joy at receiving a new pen-

---

*For more information on the Dominican Republic Cell Tech Solution, please contact Jeanne at (800) 927-2527, ext. 1695.

cil. The school children are delighted with theirs! Prior to eating Super Blue Green Algae, these same little ones were so malnourished that they would fall asleep at school and often just go home because they had no will to learn.

Now, Fernando, the orphanage director, writes, "The children are very happy. Their physical condition has generally improved. Three children, Ismael, Jo-Sue, and Oscar, were having trouble learning. They have now progressed to the next grade level."

Fernando's six children and his wife have also begun eating this wonderful life-enhancing, blue-green algae.

Though Jeanne Marie Kidd has not had the opportunity to return to Neyba to see the results of her dedication and resourcefulness, she has high hopes of doing so this year. She, and others like her, act as ambassadors for all of us in our ongoing efforts to take advantage of Daryl Kollman's window of opportunity for changing the precarious course of human destiny.

Jeanne Marie Kidd
Knoxville, Tennessee

Energia Para La Vida: "Energy for Life" The Guatemala Project

George Leger is "Our Man In Antigua." Antigua, Guatemala, that is. George is a member of a group of independent Cell Tech distributors who have banded together to support hungry people in this small Central American country. Though this ensemble of dedicated humanitarians has encountered their share of difficulties, some unbelievable coincidences convinced the group that they were on the right track.

"Serendipity," according to Webster's Dictionary, "is making fortunate and unexpected discoveries by accident." George knows about serendipity. Ever since he became involved with the children in Guatemala, he explains that he has experienced an "endless succession of coincidences, connections, and things which just come my way at the exact time I need them," just as in the encounter below. It's all seems fated somehow.

One day, in a park in Guatemala City, George met another man who was in the process of opening an orphanage on the Guatemalan coast. He had a broad vision. His dream was to provide help for all the children of Guatemala, the "street kids" as well as the orphaned ones. As the two men talked, George felt an alliance growing between them. Here was someone else with similar ideas about how to reach the needy children of this war torn, poverty ridden country.

The man pulled a pamphlet from his briefcase as he slowly turned to George. "I've received a report from Nicaragua detailing work from an organization in the United States that I really want to get in touch with. . . ." A bell went off in George's head as he took the booklet that was being handed to him. Sure enough, it was a copy of the most recent study from the Cell Tech Solution project in Nandaime, Nicaragua.

"How did you hear about this?" he asked in amazement.

"Well," explained the stranger, "a friend of mine is a Cell Tech distributor in California." He went on to say that he had read the report and wanted to find out how to secure Super Blue Green Algae for the children he would be helping. He was concerned that it might not be possible.

"It just so happens," grinned George, "that I am here to act as a representative for this company in the project they are developing here in Guatemala. It's true!" he assured the stunned man. "I have used the algae myself for four or five years, and we're involved in a two-part program to help feed, clothe, and care for the people of Guatemala. I've also just spoken with Cell Tech about making the street children a third project."

"I can hardly believe it," replied his new, like-minded friend. "I am so thrilled!"

*   *   *

The *Energia Para La Vida* (Energy for Life) project in Guatemala began in August 1992, when Cell Tech Double Diamond distributor Michael Linden met Judith Nielsen. Judith was involved with a nutritional recovery program in Guatemala for severely malnourished infants, the *Obras Sociales del Hermano Pedro* (Community Services of Brother Peter), which was founded by Dominicans in 1712. OSHP provides food and services for "infants, teenagers with [many serious health problems], castaways who are so diseased that no one wants them, and seniors with bodies that are useless vehicles for dried-up spirits." Michael immediately offered to provide Super Blue Green Algae for this project.

Other distributors, including George Leger, soon joined them to provide Super Blue Green Algae for the nutritional recovery program. Through their efforts, the Guatemalans acquired their first shipment of Alpha Sun powder through Linden and Nielsen in November 1994. Since that time, approximately one hundred patients and staff members have eaten the algae. Even with a limited supply, the recipients have noticed amazing results. Dr. Juarez, the resident pediatrician, would like to expand the program to include all 750 people at the facility.

When members of the core group of supporters visited Guatemala in July 1995, the Energy for Life project grew as they opened a second program, known as Living Waters, in Antigua. There, "Our man in Antigua," George, helps to co-ordinate six feeding sites in the area: one in Antigua, where approximately three hundred children are provided for, and five in Quiche, one of the poorest areas in the country, in which 2,500 children receive help. With only two hot meals a week available from this project, this is the only nourishment that many of the people involved receive. These feedings are the sole opportunity to give the children the much needed boost of Super Blue Green Algae.

In the area serviced by the Living Waters program, the mortality rate has fallen from 80% to approximately 15%, and the improvement in the quality of life has astounded the project workers. Under a nurse's supervision, forty of their worst cases have received a twice weekly, one teaspoon serving of algae. The nurse says that "hair is growing back, eyes are more clear and focused, skin is improving, and the people's general health and vitality is much better." In addition, there seems to be a corresponding improvement in their immune systems. Prior to eating the algae, most of the forty children experienced recurrent and persistent infections. According to George Leger, "With consistent consumption of algae, the illnesses have mostly subsided." All this with only two teaspoons per week!

Two projects still in development include the Algae Plus program in Quiche and a program that will offer help to young residents of a Harlem-like area of Guatemala City called *Zona 1*. The goal of the program in Quiche is to enhance people's lives there by encouraging them to produce their own food. Coordinators plan to become personally involved through providing expertise and tools for digging wells, planting and harvesting crops, and creating algae ponds. They will also educate the participants about the role of balanced nutrition in maintaining their health. In *Zona 1*, George's objective is to feed algae to the street kids that he has been working with for the last several years.

Many Double Diamond Distributors with Cell Tech have offered their support to the *Energia Para La Vida* program. They are a nonprofit corporation registered in the state of Maine that welcomes your inquiries and your financial contributions.

Children are our future. . . .

Michael Linden, on behalf of the Guatemala Project.

Anyone wishing for more information about the project
or to inquire about membership may write:
Guatemala Project
Box 614
Waldoboro, ME 04572
Or, you may leave a message for Michael Linden
at 1-800-746-7413.

*Information provided by Mr. Linden and presented to
Cell Tech in a formal report titled
"Energia Para la Vida: The Guatemala Project.
Overview: Genesis and Evolution," dated December 14, 1995.*

Hope L.A.

Over the last few decades, South Central Los Angeles has become an urban powder keg, threatened by quarrelling gangs and ethnic violence. Poverty abounds and hopelessness prevails. Yet amidst this bleak devastation shines a light of possibility and optimism.

Through hard work and dedication, a visionary member of the ravaged community rose above the chaos to transform an abandoned city lot into a haven of growth and tranquillity. George, the man who initiated this program, teaches these youngsters about growing food and growing healthy bodies.

Shattered only occasionally by aimless drive-by shootings, the tranquility of a burgeoning organic garden draws the local youth to wallow in the earth and heal their troubled souls. Not only does this project provide contact with Mother Nature, but it offers directionless juveniles an opportunity for a college education through scholarships and an income by marketing the produce they grow. Because nutrition is a major element of their training, most of the participants also regularly consume Super Blue Green Algae.

Cell Tech's connection with the L.A. Project began over breakfast in an upscale neighborhood in Orange County, California. Michael Stewart, a dynamic and driven Cell Tech distributor, leaned closer to his companion and spoke earnestly about his desire to help children in the United States. Michael had heard about the Nicaragua Project, which was already underway, and he felt strongly that algae should be given to underprivileged children here, too.

"Put something together, Mike, and we'll take a look at it," replied his confidant. With these words from Daryl Kollman, the L.A. Project took flight.

When Michael heard about the garden program, he contacted George immediately. Although George was already familiar with Super Blue Green Algae, he became intrigued by Michael's unique approach. Michael suggested using the algae as a soil amendment to enhance the production of high quality, organic vegetables. Then he painted a verbal picture of the health and vitality that these growing children could have if they ate the algae, too. Lastly, he presented the financial opportunity that could pave the way for their future education without reliance on welfare and government subsidies. "Give them the juice to accomplish their

> *"Michael suggested using the algae as a soil amendment..."*

goals," he encouraged. "Let's break the welfare mentality!"

Michael submitted a proposal to Cell Tech to embrace the garden project under the umbrella of the Cell Tech Solution, and within six days he had his reply. Marta Kollman called to give him the go-ahead, and his vision became reality.

Michael's perseverance and dedication created the vehicle for the development of something even greater than his original plan. "The minute I heard about George's garden project, I knew it was a done deal," he says emphatically. Another example of seeing something when you believe it, instead of the other way around!

George's vision also grows ever broader. He believes that since his community has been able to provide an opportunity for hope, health, and freedom for troubled youth, the project should be duplicated in other inner city neighborhoods across the country. New York City, Atlanta, and Connecticut are possible sites for similar garden projects.

Meanwhile, another committed individual teamed up with George to offer opportunity to the frustrated and downtrodden youth in Los Angeles. His story follows.

Information provided by Michael Stewart of Orange County, California.

Scott and Khalik Alexander

As the middle child of eight, Scott needed a strong will to be heard. From the time he was a young boy, his mother single-handedly raised her brood in crime ridden, poverty challenged South Central Los Angeles. He and his siblings scraped and scrapped their way to adulthood, resorting to stealing food from grocery stores just to survive. He carried a gun to school to protect himself from the violence that threatened to engulf him. Always a leader, never a follower, Scott refused to join one of the neighborhood gangs. He formed his own. From involvement with drugs to rumbles on the street, Scott Alexander found himself in a variety of illegal and danger-ous activities. "I got a few knocks on the head," he admits, "but I also gave a few!"

A thin ray of hope pierced the dark probability of Scott's future like a shaft of sunlight. His mother discovered Mahayana Buddhism during Scott's ninth year. He began to meditate periodically, and studied the philosophies of Bud-dhism. The transformation came slowly; the light dawned gradually. The veil of ignorance could no longer obscure the life he led or the effects of his actions in the community in which he lived.

Scott speaks slowly in a deep, molasses-rich voice, "At first, I would be a good guy one day, and the next day, some-thing would push my buttons." Though he knew what he wanted for his life, he couldn't follow through consistently. Then one day his two younger brothers met violence head on. Members of a neighborhood street gang ambushed Scott's siblings, shooting one and brutally knifing the other. Khalik, the brother who was stabbed, remained hospitalized and in a coma for two weeks, vacillating between life and death.

Scott waged battle within himself. "Do I retaliate," he won-dered, "or do I end this cycle of violence and go forward in peace?" All his studies pointed toward nonviolence and brotherhood, but Scott waited for his brothers to recover before making this important, life-changing decision.

"We chose to make a difference," Scott remembers. No longer could they perpetuate the seething rage that threatened to destroy themselves and their peers. Instead of succumbing to the turbulence and hatred around them, the brothers decided to transform their shattered community into a neighborhood free of poverty and crime. In 1992, Scott and Khalik organized the Get Loose Tribe, a nonprofit organization committed to this goal.

Later, they met another man who had dedicated his life to bringing change to the inner city of Los Angeles: George, the inner city gladiator who had spearheaded a garden project for troubled teens that offered them a chance to heal and a place to grow alongside the ripening harvest.

One day, George introduced Scott and Khalik to an "incredible food" that would provide them with the energy they needed to better accomplish their goals. Trustingly, Scott accepted the bottle of Omega Sun capsules that George handed him and innocently asked, "How many should I take?"

"Oh, take twelve," answered George. "You want to have a super start, and that should do it."

The next day, Scott and Khalik ate six algae in the morning and six in the afternoon while they worked hard to organize a room full of flea market furniture and clothing. Later that evening, as Scott wiped his gleaming ebony brow with his forearm, he asked his brother, "Have you eaten anything today?" Bursting with energy, neither of them had taken time to eat a meal, and after stopping for a quick supper, they worked on into the night. Scott knew then that he had found an amazing food.

Accustomed to dragging himself out of the bed in the morning, downing two cups of strong coffee, and languishing in a hot shower before feeling alert, Scott began to awaken so refreshed that he soon skipped the coffee. His sleep became more regular and more sound so that he no longer arose feeling tired. Since his introduction to meditation, Scott had thought of himself as patient and calm, but found that he felt even more tolerant after adding algae to his diet.

Because of his commitment to achieve financial freedom for his family and his community, Scott decided to become a Cell Tech distributor. Now, his siblings all eat algae, and so does his sixty-two year old mother. He says, "My mother is a warm Southern mama, and she's experienced so many benefits from the algae. Many of her health problems have disappeared, and she definitely has more energy. Her doctor has reduced her medication, and she's doing great!"

Scott and Khalik's organization has created a program for ex-convicts and gang members to gain control of their lives by nurturing their self-esteem and teaching them about the benefits of better nutrition through Super Blue Green Algae. With a matching scholarship from Landmark Education, they emerged from George's L.A. project and created a mentor program for people aged eighteen through thirty, with some even older. "It's a myth that gang members are all mixed-up teenagers," explains Scott. Currently, the training program serves thirty individuals, but they have enough funding for fifty.

"Spinning out of the garden project came the multilevel opportunity to empower people financially, and demonstrate the connection between nutrition and behavior," Scott asserts. "The participants have begun to think more rationally. They seem more patient and tolerant, and they have more emotional and physical stability." These are positive qualities that Scott has also observed increasingly in himself.

Scott and Khalik's dream of transforming the jungle of hopelessness and violence in South Central Los Angeles to a community of vitality and abundance is slowly becoming a reality. One step at a time, one person at a time, they bring hope, health, and freedom to a society desperate for peace.

Scott and Khalik Alexander
South Central Los Angeles

Note: Scott and Khalik Alexander are the copresidents and cofounders of the Get Loose Tribe Foundation which sponsors the L.A. Project and L.A. Story.

Network of Hope

The Network of Hope began as an idea in the mind of Double Diamond Katharine Clark. It consists of a group of independent Cell Tech distributors across North America who have a real concern for the nutritional welfare of our children. As parents, educators, and health professionals, all the members "wish to extend the window of opportunity to everyone, but are especially dedicated to helping families with school-aged children" who are learning and physically challenged in some way.

> *"Their stories, recipes, and uplifting poems provide advice and information to many parents..."*

Nearly a year in progress, the organization now includes over one hundred members in several different teams. Ten percent of the monies from its resources contribute to a variety of algae feeding programs throughout the country. Members of the Network of Hope also support cultural diversity, Distributor Empowerment Team projects,* and healthy school lunch programs. Their goal is to connect people where ever the need arises.

The Network of Hope Newsletter is published quarterly by John and Mary Votel. The subscription price is $25, of which ten percent is used to purchase algae for disadvantaged children. The Votels accept articles, poems, and insights from parents and professionals who wish to support others who have children with learning difficulties and physical challenges.

---

* Distributor Empowerment Teams are groups of Cell Tech distributors (Executive level or above) with a desire to a make a difference in their communities and in the future of the company.

Their stories, recipes, and uplifting poems provide advice and information to many parents who would otherwise have no-where to turn. If you would like to contribute to any of their programs, submit material for publication, or subscribe to the newsletter, please contact them at:

Network of Hope
P.O. Box 701534
St. Cloud, FL 34770-1534
Please send subscription monies in US funds only.

This information was submitted by
Mary Votel of St. Cloud, Florida.

5

The Company and the Products

> *You are what your deep, driving desire is.*
> *As your desire is, so is your will.*
> *As your will is, so is your deed.*
> *As your deed is, so is your destiny.*
>
> — Brihadaranyaka Upanishad IV.4.5

Cell Tech

During twelve years of teaching young children, Daryl Kollman noticed a steady drop in children's abilities to focus and concentrate, as well as an associated increase in learning problems. He related this trend to the diminishing quality of their diet. If he was to communicate with his students and have them assimilate his teaching, he needed to find a solution to this decline. Eventually, through "an extensive computer search through existing literature," Daryl found that "microalgae were being used in Japan and other Far Eastern countries for the remediation of poor educational performance in school children."*

Initially, Daryl and his wife Marta grew and harvested two types of algae, Spirulina and Chlorella, in man-made ponds in the desert of New Mexico. After an article on the Kollmans appeared in a national publication, an attorney in Klamath Falls, Oregon, contacted them about an abundance of algae growing in the nearby lake. When they received a sample of this strain of wild-grown, blue-green algae, Daryl mixed some with water and drank it to test its effectiveness for himself. Although he hadn't noticed much benefit from eating Chlorella, Daryl immediately experienced results from the new algae, and so did Marta.

Cell Tech was born in 1982 with a small harvesting site in a canal that is fed by Klamath Lake. Later, the office facility moved to an eccentric, odd-shaped building in downtown Klamath Falls, subsequently outgrowing that structure too. Along the way, the Kollmans purchased the company from their financial backers. Just recently, they signed a twenty-five year lease extension which includes exclusive harvesting rights to two additional canals. Total harvesting capacity has swelled from one or two large collection screens in the original canal to forty-seven screens overall. The company plans to construct

---

* John David Mann, "Solstice," *Upstate New York's Journal for Natural Living.* Vol. I, No. 4. (1986).

another harvesting facility directly on the lake to handle the heightened demand for more algae. The freeze-drying operation is also currently expanding to accommodate this increase.

Cell Tech's growth has been phenomenal. Throughout all these changes, they have managed to rise to the challenge, allowing them to be one of the few multilevel marketing enterprises to survive whirlwind expansion and come out on top.

The 1995 harvest yielded approximately eight million pounds of algae; the projected increase in 1996 should top forty million pounds! New equipment for bottling and encapsulating will provide the support needed to ensure a continuous supply of the harvested treasure.

From a small company that scooped up a few shovels full of algae into portable coolers, to a multimillion dollar organization with state of the art equipment and far-reaching goals, Cell Tech has blossomed into a model of business acumen and social responsibility. Much of that is due to the unceasing energy of Marta Kollman, and the vision of her husband Daryl.

Daryl's Vision

Daryl Kollman has a universal vision: increase the quality of life for every man, woman, and child on this planet. According to Daryl, we have an ever shrinking window of opportunity to make a change in the direction we are heading as a nation and as a global family. Industrial pollution, unsustainable agricultural practices, declining male fertility, severe poverty, and malnutrition all contribute to a dismal picture of our future on this planet.

Daryl quotes Mahatma Ghandi in calling our generation the "pivotal generation." He believes it is up to us to make a difference in the future of life on earth for all of our descendents. Super Blue Green Algae contributes positively to this endeavor as a potent food source for all people, as well as a means of redistributing wealth into the hands of caring, visionary individuals who will use their resources to change the course of our destiny.

We just need to reach through Daryl's window of opportunity and *seize the day*!

About the Products

With conscious intent, Cell Tech has created a very limited inventory of Super Blue Green Algae products. Because Daryl and Marta Kollman recognize the ability of this powerful food to stand on its own, they choose to maintain a pure product line without watering it down with additives and enhancements. Besides the two pure algae items, Alpha Sun and Omega Sun, only a few supportive supplements round out Cell Tech's offerings. The algae itself is available in liquid, capsule, or tablet form, as well as in scrumptious snacks called BG Bites and in three delicious smoothie flavors.

Super Blue Green Alpha Sun:
Whole algae, with the cell walls intact, are called Alpha Sun. Because of the high proportion of glycogen in the cell wall, Super Blue Green Algae is a rich energy source. It provides natural sugars critical for the health and vitality of tissues and cells.

Super Blue Green Omega Sun:
To create Omega Sun, the cell wall is carefully removed using a special *cell sonic* separation process. The result is a super-concentrated food with a higher amino acid content than Alpha Sun. It is an abundant source of raw materials for building neuropeptides that feed and enhance brain activity, thus promoting mental clarity and alertness.

Super Blue Green Liquid Omega Sun:
This is a highly concentrated extract of Omega Sun algae that is taken orally, under the tongue, with a dropper. This liquid provides the autonomic and central nervous systems with immediate nutritional fuel to function at the highest level — a truly healthy, nutritious pick-me-up without damaging side effects.

Super Blue Green Enzymes:
Derived from a plant source, Cell Tech's enzymes are microblended with 25 milligrams of Alpha Sun algae. Unlike the diet of our primitive ancestors who ate mostly raw foods, our modern diet consists of many cooked and processed foods. As a result, important enzymes are often destroyed. Super Blue Green Enzymes replaces some of these lost catalysts and is used to unlock the nutrients in our food.

Probiotics
Probiotics are helpful bacteria normally found in abundance in our digestive tracts. They assist in digestion, assimilation, and immunity and are often destroyed by environmental factors such as pollution, refined sugars, chemicals, and stress. Cell Tech offers three probiotic products:

Super Blue Green Acidophilus:
Super Blue Green Acidophilus contains an average of 1.2 billion *Lactobacillus acidophilus* in each capsule, as compared to 690 million in the Spectrabiotics. A rice-based, single-strain beneficial bacteria called DDS-1 is carefully microblended with Super Blue Green Omega Sun. The algae "turbocharges" the friendly bacteria, making the healthy bacteria grow faster and in greater numbers to colonize the small intestine and keep out harmful organisms.

Super Blue Green Bifidus:
Super Blue Green Bifidus contains at least 1.5 billion *Bifidobacterium bifidum* and 85 milligrams of Omega Sun algae in each capsule.
When the large intestine functions properly, it absorbs excess liquid from our food and passes the remaining waste out of the body. Super Blue Green Bifidus provides probiotic support by repopulating the intestinal walls with friendly bacteria, thus it may prevent gas, bloating, and diarrhea.

Spectrabiotics:
Created by world renowned nutritional scientist Dr. Khem Shahani and enzyme specialist Viktoras Kulvinskas, this prod-

uct contains seven essential enterobacteria; four digestive enzymes; Jerusalem artichoke, a source of fructo-oligosaccharides (probiotic food); and 85 milligrams of Super Blue Green Omega Sun. This provides the entire digestive tract with the most complete probiotic system ever developed. While Spectrabiotics does include acidophilus and bifidus, the concentration is smaller, and it is designed to complement these other two products.

Super Q_{10}:

While our bodies normally produce a special enzyme called Coenzyme Q_{10}, many researchers believe that our ability to create this enzyme diminishes with age and stress, eventually causing a deficiency that may contribute to disease and a weakened immune system. Super Q_{10}, which contains Super Blue Green Alpha Sun and Coenzyme Q_{10}, is the ideal way to assist the miracle of your cells in converting nutrients into energy.

Super Sprouts & Algae:

This is a unique combination with the nutritional benefits of three superfoods — organic wheat sprouts, Alpha Sun algae, and Super Red Beta, a premium strain of saltwater algae. Together, they supply the body with an extraordinary storehouse of superior antioxidant nutrition to neutralize the effects of highly unstable, reactive molecules known as freeradicals which contribute to premature aging and cellular degeneration.

BG Bites:

These chewy snacks are made from all natural ingredients including raisins, dates, malt syrup, and Super Blue Green Alpha Sun algae. They are available in three delicious flavors: Raspberry, Toasted Almond, and Sesame. They are a wonderful way for children and adults to obtain Super Blue Green nutrition in a convenient, portable package. Great for school lunches!

Super Sun Smoothies:
With 500 milligrams each of Alpha and Omega Sun blended into every scoop, Super Sun Smoothies mix with your favorite beverage or fresh fruit to make a refreshing, nutritious shake. This all-vegetable powder is made with premium ingredients; it's dairy free, and contains no sugar, preservatives, yeast, artificial flavoring or coloring. Smoothies come in Banana, Vanilla, and Strawberry flavors, and provide approximately fifteen servings in each can.

Super Blue Green Algae for Animals:
A finely processed powder, Super Blue Green Algae for Animals may be mixed in with your pet's regular food or sprinkled liberally on top. It is suitable for all animals — from goldfish to cats and dogs, even horses. If at any time you are unable to obtain this product, the regular line of algae items can be used for animals.

Rivers of Light Skin and Hair Care System:
Cell Tech carries a limited line of skin care products as well as a shampoo and conditioner made from natural products combined with crystalline pure Rivers of Light spring water. They contain no solvent alcohol, artificial perfumes, mineral oils, artificial colors, or animal derivatives of any kind.

Eat Algae Today (EAT) Kit:
The EAT kit contains Super Blue Green Spectrabiotics, a large bottle of Super Blue Green Enzymes, and one bottle each of Omega Sun and Alpha Sun capsules. The package also supplies a comprehensive progress journal for recording health changes, an informative audiocassette about each of the products and how to begin the program, a fold-out product guide, and an algae key-chain carrier (for toting your algae with you during the day). This complete package is an ideal way to begin eating Super Blue Green Algae, as it contains the digestive aids that are so important for the proper assimilation of the algae. Instructions and information are clear and concise, and the progress journal provides an ongoing record of

changes in your health. Super Q^{10} and Super Sprouts & Algae may be added to this basic program as needed.

Please contact an independent Cell Tech distributor to obtain a comprehensive order guide and ongoing support with your Super Blue Green Algae products.

Biography

Born in a small company hospital on the Mediterranean island of Cyprus, Dr. Lisa Moore obtained a rich and varied education from attending school in England and Lebanon, as well as from digging in her own backyard. The urge to explore uncharted territory led her to chiropractic college in Davenport, Iowa. Although a less exotic location, it also held the keys to an esoteric wisdom.

Lisa continually explores new and different avenues for physical, emotional, and spiritual transformation. This pursuit brought her to an exciting development in her own profession: Network Spinal Analysis. She now utilizes this approach exclusively while also including whole food nutrition such as Super Blue Green Algae.

Her chiropractic office is located in the Sierra foothills of Northern California, where she lives with her two algae-eating children and her three algae-eating cats. Lisa plans to create books on other health-related subjects in the future. "Teaching comes naturally," she says. "Imparting information is a necessary component of being a physician. The word *doctor* means *teacher*, and that is a sacred trust for me."

Lisa is currently writing a second book about individuals who have succeeded in building a new life for themselves through the Cell Tech business opportunity. If you have achieved hope, health, and freedom by telling others about Super Blue Green Algae, please write to her care of Ransom Hill Press, PO Box 325 Ramona, CA, 92065, or call her Concord voice mail box at 1-800-927-2527 ext. 1036.

Important
Telephone Numbers:

Cell Tech Order Line:
1-800-800-1300

Cell Tech FAX Order Hotline:
1-800-797-8228

Cell Tech Automated 24 Hour Order Hotline:
1-800-800-6069

Cell Tech Distributor Services:
1-541-883-8848

Cell Tech Distributor Services FAX Line:
1-541-884-1869

> To order Cell Tech Super Blue Green Algae, please contact the person who gave you this book or call Cell Tech's Distributor Services to find a Cell Tech representative near you.

For more information about Network Chiropractic/
Network Spinal Analysis, please contact:
The Association for Network Chiropractic
444 North Main Street
Longmont, CO 80501.
Or telephone at (303) 678-8101.

Algae Related Books and Audios Available From Ransom Hill Press

#AS   Fifty Algae Stories,* *Lisa C. Moore, DC* $12.95

#CC   **Complicated Child? Simple Options,***
Becki Linderman $10.00

#AR   **Algae to the Rescue,** *Karl Abrams* $14.95

#RE1   **The Regeneration Effect I:** Spearheading Regeneration
with Wild Blue Green Algae, (Previously titled The
Genesis Effect), *Dr. John Apsley II* $8.95

#RE2   **The Regeneration Effect II:** A Professional Treatise on
Self Healing, *Dr. John Apsley II* $19.95

#GEN GENAPSUR computer software for Windows monitors
bodily changes while eating blue green algae $19.95
#GENS (Regeneration Effect II & Software) .... set @ $29.95

#RE3   **The Regeneration Effect III:** Super Brain Function and
Restoration, Attention Deficit Disorder, *Dr. John Apsley II* $12.95

#CQ   **The Miracle Nutrient Coenzyme Q10,**
Emile Bliznakov, MD $6.50

#DMT/B   Big D's Little d's for a Lifetime of Health,*
Dr. J. Ronald Meyers....Audio Cassette....$3.00, Booklet $3.50

#SC   **Simple, Cheap and Easy:** How to Build A Cell Tech
Business Off Your Kitchen Table,* *Venus Andrecht* $9.95

Volume Discounts on TWO or more items!

Ransom Hill Press carries other titles on health, nutrition and
network marketing, as well as audio cassettes, postcards,
T-shirts and gift items.

For your FREE catalog or to order any books listed here, call Ransom Hill Press at:

☎ **Voice: 1-800-423-0620**
FAX: 619-789-1582

* Published by Ransom Hill Press
Prices subject to change without notice.

Featured Titles

Simple, Cheap and Easy:
How To Build A Cell Tech Business Off Your Kitchen Table
Venus Andrecht
Item #SCE $9.95

Simple, Cheap and Easy teaches you everything you need to know to make your Cell Tech business thrive! It was written *just* for Cell Tech distributors, and leads you step-by-step through the process of approaching people with the algae and then quickly signing them as distributors.

Complicated Child?
Simple Options
Becki Linderman
Item #CC $10.00

Revised with new updates!
"Let me begin by sharing my personal story with you. . ." writes Becki Linderman in this heartwarming and hope-giving book. Read of the transformations that learning and behaviorally challenged children have experienced after adding Super Blue Green Algae to their diets. Listen as parents discuss how their family has changed and grown in wonderfully unexpected ways thanks to the alternative they found in SBG algae.

Big D's Little d's
For A Lifetime of Health
Dr. J. Ronald Meyers
Item #DM $3.00 sample cassette.

☛The best audiotape for consumers we've ever heard!
☛ Dr. Meyers gives his patients compelling reasons why they should eat blue-green algae for the rest of their lives.
☛ A former professor, Dr. Meyers gives you easy to understand, "carry around" information so you can easily explain why the algae is so important. Or, let the tape do your talking!

Call for volume discounts.